—— STORIES ——

EATING HABITS OF THE CHRONICALLY LONESOME

D1737040

MEGAN GAIL COLES

© 2014, Megan Gail Coles

Canada

We gratefully acknowledge the financial support of the Canada Council for the Arts, the Government of Canada through the Canada Book Fund (CBF), and the Government of Newfoundland and Labrador through the Department of Tourism, Culture and Recreation for our publishing program.

Printed on acid-free paper
Cover Design by Jud Haynes
Layout by Tracy Harris

Published by
KILLICK PRESS
an imprint of CREATIVE BOOK PUBLISHING
a Transcontinental Inc. associated company
P.O. Box 8660, Stn. A
St. John's, Newfoundland and Labrador A1B 3T7

Printed in Canada

Library and Archives Canada Cataloguing in Publication

Coles, Megan, author
Eating habits of the chronically lonesome / Megan Gail Coles.

Short stories.
ISBN 978-1-77103-052-6 (pbk.)

I. Title.

PS8605.O4479E28 2014   C813'.6   C2014-904696-0

STORIES

EATING HABITS OF THE CHRONICALLY LONESOME

killick press
an imprint of Creative Publishers

St. John's, Newfoundland and Labrador
2014

For Maria, Katie, Bethany and Kelly.

EATING HABITS OF THE CHRONICALLY LONESOME

THERE ARE TEARS
IN THIS COCONUT

A painted blonde child of about six is crying to my Thai masseuse. Coral lipstick is smudged across her face while blue mascara runs trenches down her fat cheeks. The masseuse comforts the girl in Thai and I'm surprised when she nods her head in response. The child's features take on a new Asian quality as I search for a family resemblance. The pair becomes distracted by someone approaching to our left. I arch my neck to peer from beneath the umbrella. I was initially annoyed by the interruption. A screaming child is not relaxing. But now I'm intrigued.

A six-foot-plus figure approaches, quietly scolding the child in German. A long tangerine sarong hides larger than female calves, a lilac halter betrays clearly masculine shoulders. So this person, the father, has obviously chosen to live as a woman. Koa Samui doesn't seem to mind. Koa Samui seems to mind very little, in fact. The girl is passed along to her daddy-mommy. She wraps her slender tan arms around the German's neck and pushes back a swarm of frizzy curls to clear space for her soaked cheek. The scene is calm now. Affectionate. An elementary-style storm averted by parental attentions. A completely trilingual conversation occurs and I'm jealous. The child and her daddy-mommy lean in to kiss my masseuse. He-she utters an apology to me before walking back down the beach. Everyone and their dog speaks English here. My massage resumes.

And I deserve a massage. I deserve Koa Samui, air-conditioning and a double bed to myself. I'm splurging on the comforts of the Western world in an Eastern paradise. I may even get my nails painted. Leanne would hate that. She would lecture me on hygiene, oppression, and self-reliance. Leanne is forever blathering on about hepatitis. It's her new favourite subject now. That and humanitarian projects. Her ex-husband's homosexuality has suddenly transformed her into a benevolent pain in my ass. I don't know why I agreed to this.

I know exactly why I agreed to this.

I agreed to this because my older sister was crying on the living room floor, dry heaving into a bread pan after drinking every night for three weeks. Leanne was hysterical by dinnertime. She was never eating. She was all dirty hair and loud phone calls, as she sat in the kitchen sink smoking out the window. Leanne didn't smoke. She was miserable and hopeless. I hated seeing her like that. She had always been overwhelming, even as a happily married woman. But this was entirely different. I thought she was losing her mind. I would return after a night of dancing to find her delirious on the couch, empty beer bottles all over the house. A depressing treasure hunt revealing half-eaten poutine and broken picture frames. Sometimes she would be ordering magazines, screaming, *Fuck Trevor, I can get my own fucking reading material!* Or sometimes she would be stalking him on the computer, listing every gay man he had ever acted opposite. *Do you think he fucked Jimmy when they were in* Lear *last year? Or Frank when they did* Mother Courage *at Factory?* Always. Radiohead. Blasting.

Then she discovered Dave's ESL and the world. She started bathing again. She bought vegetables. Leanne was scheming and I knew it. I had seen that look in her eye every time she went to bed early in high school. When she switched her major to theatre. When she introduced us to her scene study partner, Trevor. Leanne was scheming something, but I didn't care because at least she was back to being her tricky self. At least I knew how to deal with that.

—

Clare wasn't at the bungalow when Leanne got back. Though, she could hardly tell. Her sister's side of the room is so messy, you can barely notice things missing. But there were signs. Leanne's Swiss Army knife had disappeared, which made opening a bottle of wine impossible. Clare's hikers weren't emanating their usual stench from the doorway, and the dandruff shampoo wasn't in the shower. Probably off to bitch about Leanne to the other useless vagrants that call themselves *volunteers*. Not that Leanne was surprised her little sister would take up with the beach bums. She had always behaved like a surfer who had never been to California. Clare. Never combing her hair as a child. Clare. Always eating food over the sink. Leanne is certain Clare doesn't want her to be happy, that she prefers Leanne in crisis. The whole family does. They can pretend like they're some sort of proper, supportive family when Leanne can barely dress herself. But are they supportive when things are going well? Nope. Then it's, *Leanne is so selfish. Leanne only calls when she wants something. Leanne's temper is retarded.*

Really, this is all Trevor's fault. That fag. Pretending he loved her. Marrying Leanne in front of their families. In front of God. An abomination. Or it would be if Leanne believed in God. Or if there had been a priest. Whatever. It's still an abomination to marry a woman when you would rather suck a cock. Leanne would never have had to move in with her little sister if he hadn't, if he wasn't.... Leanne doesn't hate gay men, she just hates one gay man. Saying he just wasn't a sexual person. That he preferred intimacy. That he wanted to be friends. Jesus. Leanne feels like a proper idiot.

Clare's an idiot too, though. Can't be bothered to pick her clothes up off the bathroom floor. Would never think to scrape a plate. So what if Leon sleeps over? Leanne suspects Clare has already called Mom and Dad crying. They'll probably give her money, worry about her safety, her sanity. Probably blame everything on Leanne. A family tradition. Sure, they'd leave Leanne to rot in prison, all the while claiming that they were teaching her some kind of a lesson; *Brokedown Palace* style. Independence. Her mother would say something about tough love while her father listed off her numerous past offences. The time she sold her furniture for pot. The time she maxed out a credit card. The time she failed math. As if Leanne was the only twenty-year-old to ever have the gall to fail math. Clare failed math. And it wasn't even mentioned for fear it would upset her fragile self-esteem.

Clare doesn't have fragile self-esteem. It's all an elaborate ruse.

Like when she says she only came to Thailand for her sister's mental health. Yeah. She neglects to mention that she failed out of U of T. Fucking forgot that relevant fact. Anyway, Leanne paved the way for her. Clare should be grateful. She should bow down to Leanne for breaking every rule while she was still playing with her dollies. That's why Clare had it so easy. Why their parents are so attentive and concerned, cause they fucked Leanne up. She's a lost cause. Their guinea pig. But does Clare say thank you? Does she show an ounce of appreciation? No. Of course not. Instead she runs off knowing full well Leanne will freak out. *I don't need you to worry about me. I already have a mother. I can take care of myself.* Fine. Leanne decides she won't worry. Let Clare take care of herself. See how far she gets with her mediocre Thai.

—

And Leanne wants us to learn Thai now. All up in my face because I don't spend enough time studying. My language skills aren't improving, she says, while she slathers sunblock on her knees. She's always putting sunblock on her knees. Language skills. Skin damage. Housework. She's a tyrant! Who can travel with a tyrant? Leanne. Always moving my stuff. Leanne. Never sitting still. No wonder she's so damn skinny. And she's a furnace. Those first two months I thought I would smother sleeping next to her. Leanne's clammy limbs spread wide. Her boozy morning breath in my face. Oblivious to how her separation was causing me sleepless nights. Always in need of constant affection. Always in need of reassurance. *Of course you didn't turn him gay. He was always gay.* Sure, anyone could see that. Trevor. Taking so much interest in Leanne's clothing. Trevor. Buying a straightening iron for himself. He was practically on fire. But you can't tell Leanne anything. She knows best, knows everything about everyone, everything. Leanne carries a soapbox around in her backpack which is, of course, immaculate. Fucking sister. Wanted to go to Africa first. To help, she said. To make something of her life, she said. I thought, Africa doesn't need help from lonely thirty-two-year old divorcees. Instead, I said that Africa didn't have enough food for the Africans. Leanne said she wouldn't eat very much.

So I agreed to go to Thailand. And here I am trying to wash fucking sunblock out of my eyes with a garden hose.

In Koa Toa. Alone in a bungalow at night that has no electricity. I have never slept in full darkness alone before. Not darkness like this. I can't see anything. The mosquito net smells bad. Like cigarette smoke and other people's sex. And I can hear things moving outside. Above me. Below me. Snakes. Snakes are most certainly surrounding my barely risen bunk in this barely risen cabin. A shack really. I think about all the snakes in this jungle country and start to cry because I will most definitely wake up not alive. Or worse. Covered in snakes. I promise myself to never trust Leanne ever again. She never keeps her promises. First promise broken: it'll be a dream vacation. Second promise broken: it won't be very expensive. Third promise broken: it'll be just us.

But it isn't a dream. It's little girls having their bodies pressed against buildings by middle-aged European perverts. And starving tigers chained to the side of cliffs so tourists can take their pictures. It's swollen bug bites, sand in my vagina, nasty hangovers and hot garbage. It's expensive. And it isn't just us.

Leon. If that is his real name. Seems a bit suspicious to me. Sounds a lot like Leanne. Coincidence or con man? Leon sleeps in our bungalow all the time. He eats our food and uses our shower. I tell him, I say, *This is not England, buddy. There isn't an infinite amount of hot water here.* And he laughs and mumbles some British nonsense that he thinks is charming. He whips his wet hair around, his hair water dripping on my skin. Huh. They've discovered Bob Marley. They're both reading the same book. They feed each other lobster-flavoured potato chips and whisper. I could vomit. I could die.

It's not that I'm not happy for her. I am. Happy for her. But this was supposed to be our trip. Our sister vacation. Not Leanne, Clare and Leon. And Leon's giant, perfect, white smile that he whores around twenty-four hours a day. No one is genuinely that happy. Looking at Leanne like he's going to eat her. They're insufferable. I can't wait to get back to Toronto where no one smiles or makes eye contact.

—

Leanne goes to that mangy hut they call the "Tsunami Relief Centre" to find Clare. She has been volunteering there since they arrived in Khao Lak. It stinks of beer farts and marijuana. Leanne doesn't know what Clare sees in these useless space vampires. Her little sister doesn't even do drugs. Clare thinks Leanne is too harsh. That she is being *overly judgmental*. Regardless, Leanne has no time for self-righteous hippies from Vancouver, who pretend to help when all they really do is get drunk and spread chlamydia. No wonder the people here resent them. The Relief Centre staff say they haven't seen Clare all week. That they just assumed she had gone on a *sojourn* and Leanne is beyond annoyed. Firstly, she finds it irritating when Anglos throw random French words into sentences to communicate their worldliness. Bullshit. Leanne calls bullshit on their French words. And secondly, what kind of sham are they running here? Clare hasn't shown up for over a week and no one thinks to contact her family? Leanne conveys her displeasure to them in a random bout of expletives. She has been trying not to curse in Thailand, figuring Trevor has likely earned every curse word she owns for the rest of her life. Apparently, there are quite a few not reserved for him after all. He sent her an email Tuesday past that said he might be bisexual. That he is in an open relationship with his director and leading lady at Stratford. He says, he finds it all very emotionally satisfying. He's feeling artistically fulfilled. He wanted Leanne to know this because he is embracing honesty. Now. He has chosen to embrace honesty, now. Now, that he's ruined her life.

The girl, because she is a girl, twenty-one tops, lectures Leanne on introducing negative energy into the space. She wears a white, orange, and pink scarf tied around her head. It is not a Southeast Asian purchase. It is high-quality, pure silk, Western fare. And Leanne sees in that instant who this girl is: casually mentioning over spicy tuna rolls in an upscale Kitsalano eatery, that maybe she'd like to go volunteer in Thailand. Youthful parents handing her their credit card. Telling her they love her. Be safe, they say. Later, they congratulate one another on their selfless daughter over glasses of champagne in the rooftop hot tub. Oh darling, we are doing such a fabulous fucking job. Best parents ever.

Leanne thinks she will strangle this girl if she does not produce Clare. Leanne is suddenly leaning across the desk, wearing her father's crazy eyes, demanding answers, making threats. She is what Clare calls *running hot* right now. But this girl, this Erica, doesn't know anything. Knows nothing. She is shiny and empty and an utter waste of Leanne's time. And now Leanne starts to worry—pacing, smoking, swearing. Leon's attempts to comfort her are in vain. Because everything that happens around her is insignificant. Barefoot twin ten-year-olds make change for her soda at a roadside stall and she feels nothing for them. An old beggar woman holding an infant pleads, No mama, no papa, please, no mama, no papa. And she feels nothing. The heat, the dirt, the hunger, the need. The grief of all these desperate people surrounding Leanne means nothing because she does not know where her little sister is. Leanne calls their mother to confess and the conversation quickly crumbles into hysterical I'm-sorrys. A symphony of I-don't-knows.

Don't come home without your sister, her mother says, and hangs up.

—

I find my way to Hat Rin. I am lavish with my remaining baht. I go to the bank in Thong Sala with the intent to spend what remains of my savings before heading back to Canada. I save just enough for the ferry and bus to Bangkok, food and shelter, and my flight. If I need to, I will call Mom and Dad and ask for money. I will tell them how awful Leanne has been if they start to chastise me. I spend my first day lying on the beach reading the *Da Vinci Code*. Leanne would despise it. She has been snatching it out of my hands for months. She thinks it will rot my mind. She is a consummate snob in everything she does. She won't even talk to the volunteers at the centre. Not that I blame her. I didn't want to hang out with those people either. I didn't have a choice. I wouldn't have hung out with them if Leanne wasn't busy every day and night with fucking Leon. He even tried to set me up with one of his friends. A pity fuck to get me out of their hair. Asshole.

I say, asshole, out loud as a woman my age approaches. She puts her towel down next to mine and explains that she needs to sit by me to discourage a leering tanned man's advances. He doesn't look pleased. Or Asian. Her name is Annetta. She is Polish and travelling alone. I have bits of butter and corn on my face. I eat corn on a stick a lot in Thailand. I love eating things on sticks. Annetta is lean and tanned with long white-blonde hair. She tells me she installs hair extensions in London. That is why her English is so good. But her dream is to be a ski instructor in Alberta. I am relieved to talk to someone. Later we go for dinner and drinks. It's like I am on a girl date. I am so pleased to have a friend. Annetta wants to go to a foam party. I am tired and unsure, but I am also determined to have fun on my vacation. When will I ever go to Asia again, right? So I go with her and it's fun. The soapy water soaks the money in my pocket and I'm pleased I left most of it in my room. We say good night and go to our separate bungalows.

I've just laid my wet baht on the foot of my bed when Annetta knocks on my door. She has a bottle of wine. She says the stars are wonderful, so I go drink more. I get even more drunk. I try to leave before the wine is finished but Annettta is adamant. She is confiding in me about her childhood in Poland and I feel obligated to stay. When I finally crawl the length of the beach to my bungalow, the door has been kicked in. I am instantly sober and start to panic. My screaming brings the front-desk man down. He calls the police. They explain to me that there is a group of foreign men robbing young women in the area. The Handsome Man Gang. They are from Columbia and they have stolen everything. My passport, my camera, my iPod, and all my baht. The few wet dollars remain spread out on my bed. A reminder of happier times. And I turn on Annetta. She is standing nodding her head at the police as they explain stolen items are rarely recovered. Almost never. I grab her and yell, You! I accuse her of setting me up. Of keeping me away. Of robbing me. And she smirks in her superior European way. As if I'm stupid. And she tells me to grow up. So I punch her in the face.

—

Leanne calls a girl from high school who works at a bank on Bay Street. This girl, now woman, drives a pearl white BMW and owns a cottage on the lake. Leanne has been avoiding her and everyone like her for years. They represent the ordinary person she was. They represent the things that an ordinary person wants. It shames Leanne that she still wants these ordinary things. The now-woman asks after Trevor. Of course she does. She knows. Everyone knows. And why let that opportunity pass. Leanne informs her that he is at Stratford with his boyfriend and girlfriend. And of course, they are still in contact. They are soulmates. Let the now-woman and the other yogis chew on that over their two glasses of white wine. Leanne explains about Clare and her voice breaks as she asks for the favour. Thankfully, family trumps pettiness. Clare has used her bankcard in Thong Sala.

Leon worries that Leanne is not eating enough to live. He says he has never before met a woman who can survive on nicotine and guilt alone. But Leanne can only sit on her single bed, back against the wall, staring at Clare's single bed across the room and smoke. Leon tries to comfort her, She's angry. You fought. She'll come back. He says, he hates to see her cry. And Leanne is standing in the middle of the room pronouncing all the reasons why her family is right. It is her fault. All of it. She never listens. Never studied in school, got shit grades, and a useless theatre degree. She is a mediocre actress at best. Directors say she doesn't work well with others and her bone structure is all wrong for television. She bullied her hot boyfriend into becoming her hot husband, and he finally left her to be with other hot men when she tried to bully him into having kids. Then she convinced her baby sister to go to Thailand and lost her. Tears are a steady stream running down Leanne's face as Leon walks toward her. He slowly lifts her dress. Pulls her panties. Buries his face. This is the only way he knows to make her feel better. But she stands there and feels worse. She pulls him up toward her and says, no. And says just one word more before leaving, says, Clare.

Clare. With chicken pox on her first birthday. Clare. Mimicking Michelle from *Full House*. Crying at the movies. Loving big cats and all kinds of rodents. Clare. Worshipping Leanne before she somehow lost her trust.

Leanne does not call their parents. She has decided she will not call them again until she finds her little sister. She will never go home. She will die looking. She arrives at Koa Pha-Ngan with a poor- quality photo of Clare on printer paper. She walks from bungalow operation to bungalow operation. No one knows. Or cares. Their lives are hard enough to occupy their time. Leanne goes to the Hat Rin Police Station before looking for somewhere to sleep. She shows them the photo of her sister. A young officer leaves momentarily and returns with a manila envelope. He opens it and carefully urges passports onto the counter. A dark corner catches Leanne's attention. And there she is. Hair not combed. Not smiling. Because she's not supposed to. Clare.

EVERYONE EATS WHILE I STARVE TO DEATH HERE

Damon thinks, this, everything, is Brenda Hann's fault for making him believe her pussy was made of gold. False advertising if there has ever been such a thing. Brenda and her tea-cup tits whispering in his ear about the big money to be made in Alberta. He was missing the rush, thousand-dollar signing bonuses at Tim Hortons, she said. Ms. Loyalty herself abandoned him in Montreal as soon as she found out his bank account balance. What did he think? she said. She was going to foot the bill? Damon had thought that. He thought they were in love. That old tea-cup tits would be the mother of his children. He thought they would get jobs, buy a house, leave St. John's and Newfoundland, obligation and poverty, behind them. But that's not what Brenda had in mind. This he discovered when he woke up on her brother Garry's couch.

Yeah, Brenda took off.
What? When?
Last night after you got shitfaced. But don't worry b'y. You can sleep here 'til you straightens yourself out. Just feed yourself.

Damon shakes his head as he walks through Berri Metro

11

toward the green line. Thinking back, he is aware that he fucked himself over taking up with the likes of Brenda Hann after his mother warned him not to. He knew he couldn't expect to go back. Sitting there on Garry Hann's garbage couch, staring blankly at Garry Hann's shitty television, aware that even Garry Hann had more than he did at the moment. Damon had gotten drunk before leaving town, had told everyone on Water Street to go fuck themselves, to rot in it, while he went off to get some of that Alberta money. He may have even took a shit in the street to punctuate this last point. Jesus. So going home was not really an option. Nope. He thought about becoming a homeless person, perhaps taking up heroin or something that would warrant his downward spiral. Instead, Garry Hann found him a job.

Now, listen buddy. Beggars can't be choosers so I don't want to hear anything out of you but gratitude.

Damon didn't think there would be anything to complain about until he realized his job at McGill required him to sort body parts all day long. Arms in one pile, legs in another. All day long in the med school fridge sorting through the pieces of unfortunates who felt science deserved their rotting corpses more than the earth. He would never donate his shit to science so that some over-privileged bitch from Niagara could discover the inner workings of his elbow. Fuck that altogether. And they were all bitches too. Walking around smelling so clean, better soap than his own Ivory, better shampoo than his own Pert Plus. Damon was sure these girls used only salon products, wore only designer labels and farted scents inspired by the Body Shop. Good Lord, didn't he want to screw them all, but they didn't even notice him. He was just another hired hand.

Dame, you think those med school girls gives good head?
Jesus if I know.
I bet they sucks a mean cock on account of their intricate knowledge of the penis.

Now that's all Damon can think about when the med students come by for their props. He pictures them all sucking each other off while surrounded by miscellaneous limbs. Girl-boy, boy-boy, girl-girl. Pictures them using some poor dead fucker's hands as knee pads. Everyone getting off, screwing into the night like lab rats. Everyone but him. Damon wasn't totally ignorant about the habits of these scholars either. He didn't come to this perverse impression on his own. Didn't have to because he actually shared a wall with one of them, a guy named Ian who never once asked him over for a beer. Ian fancied himself a guitar player. This long haired nancy-boy thought himself some great maverick. His academic prowess only overshadowed by his ability to drag random wannabe Indie chicks home from the Barfly on any given night. Oh Ian, the original Casanova, would get these nameless, giggling airheads home and fuck them on the desk against the wall that he shared with Damon. This was almost always preceded by an off key rendition of John Mayer's *Your Body is a Wonderland.*

Major Turd hauled another one home last night.
Go on. That guy's ball sack must be rubbed raw.
Whatever.
Wonder how he affords to go out on the party all the time.
I don't know but I'll never forgive Karma if I ever finds out that shit is independently wealthy.
Yes b'y.

Garry could relate. He spent most of his weeknights at home on his shitty couch eating cold clam chowder from a can, after which he would amuse himself with the provocative CTV lineup. Garry's love life involved pulling himself off to the American Apparel ads on the back of the *Montreal Mirror.* Montreal's premier arts rag, apparently.

It's perfect for me. Free and there's a new one every Thursday.

The reason Garry did these things was 'cause he couldn't

afford any better. Half of what he earned over at Pretty Paws was carted off to Newfoundland. Child support for an autistic kid he had with Slutty Marie down Gilbert Street, this the result of a one-night stand.

Have you ever heard a sadder story, Dame? I mean, really? I barely poked her. We weren't even lying down. It's like her body sucked me sperm right up inside her that night, vacuum cunt on her. Don't ever have a go at the neighbourhood whore in an alley. Nothing good will come of it.

Of course, Garry didn't mean that. He loved the little fellow. He just found it really hard to be around him because of how special he was.

The little fellow's a bit picky, too hey? Some days he'll only eat stuff that's brown, other days he'll only eat stuff that's yellow. You've got to find out what colour he's into before you does the shopping. Got a real strong memory though. Photographic.

Too bad Garry couldn't remember to make his child support payments on time. If he had, perhaps he wouldn't be receiving phone calls from Slutty Marie in the middle of the night. Garry wouldn't owe Slutty Marie $2600.0 in back payments if he had a better memory. Or if the owner of Pretty Paws paid him near what he was worth. The owner felt $12.50 an hour was more than enough for some Anglo to shave cats. That's what Garry did: he was the puss shaver. Scratches all over his arms, slight painful cat scratches that were stained from the constant iodine baths. Garry was terrified of needles and believed iodine would save him from one in the event that one of these kitties had rabies. And he was sure they all had rabies considering the way they jerked and screeched when he turned on the clippers. Sometimes the cat moaning got so much that he started to pray silently. He wondered whether a cat could be possessed by the devil. Garry was convinced it would happen to him if it was, in fact, possible.

Go on, Garry. No cat wants to be shaved. It's a normal reaction.

But if it could happen...I mean, I'm pretty unlucky. Do you know how many other guys from the West End tapped Slutty Marie in that alley? Shit loads. She only has one kid, man, mine.

Things carried on this way for quite some time. Damon in the freezer playing head, shoulders, knees and toes with the help of an extra set of arms. He amused himself for hours with foolish little games like this. He pretended to be a gay steward for a week, using the arms to lengthen his In-Case-of-an-Emergency speech. Meanwhile, Garry was working overtime at Pretty Paws. He was expanding his career options by learning how to dye the cats. White cats were especially susceptible to the dye and most owners were just interested in a "dip" meaning Garry "dipped" the cat's tail into a vat of neon, deep, some, whatever, colour.

Spends sixty bucks to get the cat's tail made pink. Dips 'em like a custard cone, I do.

Sixty bucks, that's what I spend on groceries.

I know, man, I know. But they got more money than God.

Life sucks.

Not for everyone.

Garry still couldn't manage to make his child support payments even with the extra money he was making untangling cats. Slutty Marie, who was secretly hoping he would move home and proclaim his undying love for her, decided her approach was not getting the results she desired.

That crazy bitch down the street won't let Ma see the young fellow. Says he's sick all the time but Aunt Syb seen him outside playing with his kite just yesterday. Ma's right upset over it. Now I got two of them calling me, wailing into the phone. I'm gonna go cracked, b'y. I knows it.

Wish I could help you out my man but you knows I don't have a cent.

Damon wouldn't have lent Garry money even if he'd had some. He still harboured a state of resentment towards Brenda and this bled over into his relationship with Garry even though he pretended that he'd lay his life down for the man. This he felt he had to do, considering Garry was the only person in Montreal he could call. Damon had always been somewhat of a loner but in St. John's there were always any number of people at the bar you knew in some way. Friends for the evening, your drinking buddy for the night, no questions asked the next day. Damon had tried this in Montreal a few times but found that the guys would always ask him for his number, call him around noon to see if he was interested in lunch. Lunch? Damon mistook the first guy for a homosexual and apologized for leading him on.

I'm not gay, I just wanted to know if you were hungry.

Damon decided he wasn't hungry. Definitely not hungry. Definitely hungover. Why go out anyway? He didn't even know this guy, what were they supposed to talk about? The second time this happened he promised to never give his number out again, but then he got drunk and did. The third time this happened he decided that he would only drink with Garry Hann from now on. Garry was never hungry after a night of hard drinking' cause he couldn't afford to be.

Slutty Marie called. Says the young fellow needs to go see some specialists in Halifax. I told her to have a card game.

Have a card game? Marie wasn't having no card game. She was trying to convince Garry that he couldn't make it on the mainland without saying so. She didn't want Garry Hann pissed off at her, she loved Garry Hann. Had loved him since he wore a short tie to a dance in grade nine. She thought he was the best-looking and most brazen young fellow in their entire high school, Newfoundland, maybe the world. She was right gone on him. But he didn't even give her a look. She was just that girl from down the road, one of Brenda's little friends. Her tits weren't big enough and her ass wasn't hard enough. The boys didn't even notice her until she decided to make it impossible for them to ignore her. Overnight Brenda's little friend down Gilbert Street transformed herself into Slutty Marie: super skank. She had sex in sheds, alleys, behind light poles, up against the gym doors, she was everywhere and nowhere at once. She was soaped, scented and so easy that everyone was lining up to get her attention. When finally Garry Hann looked in her direction, she made sure to take an extra large bite out of that condom wrapper. There was no way she was planning on spreading her legs for all those losers again. Yuck, b'y.

So the plan was a result of the last phone call Garry accepted from his mother, claiming that Marie would rather pay a babysitter than send the young fellow over with her. Poor Mother Hann was in no state to be calling collect. She could barely get her words out with all the screeching and hiccupping she was doing into the receiver.

She working nights now, Garry, sending the little fellow off with some stranger. Well, not, not, not really stranger I suppose, but that Rita. Sure, all her youngsters is in jail Garry. Jail! We don't want the little fellow wit her, do we? I mean, I don't know what she did to her own youngsters, but Garry, they're not right, not one of them. I never gets to spend any time with him, Garry. No youngsters around. I'm so lonely. Sometimes I thinks I'm gonna die.

This brought tears to his eyes as he stood next to the motoring refrigerator straining to hear her words over the incessant hum. Garry didn't want to hear his mother sound so desperate on his dime. He didn't want to think about Slutty Marie using his money to pay some babysitter, and he certainly didn't want to think about what his ma was cooking while she wailed away at him. Garry was opening a can of tuna, again, with his Swiss Army knife. The slow tears running down his face were for his mother, his young fellow, his situation and one part for whatever was swimming in his mother's stew pot. Garry promised he would talk to Slutty Marie, he would straighten things out. He told his mother to expect the boy off the bus the next evening. Marie wasn't so easily convinced.

No, Gar. No. You needs to send me that money you owes me.

Jesus, Marie. It's his grandmother. The boy should spend nights with family members not with some random woman.

He should spend nights with his mother. Or his father but he can't cause his father is useless.

Marie...don't get like that. I'm doing the best I can.

I bet you are. Living the high life in great big Montreal.

I'm eating dinner from a tin can, Marie! Christ. How's that high?

Yeah, well. Money would go a lot further if you lived here at home.

Home? What? Your home?

No...no. I didn't say that. I mean, home Newfoundland home.

Listen, Marie. What if I said I'd get you the money by next week? Would you let the boy go over to Ma's tomorrow or what?

How you going get money if you're so poor?

You never mind how. Just...send the young fellow over to Mother's. Jesus, Jesus.

Which is what led to Garry visiting Damon at work the very next day. A lunch date with tuna sandwiches. A proposition. The proposition. And Damon was desperate. He was sick of eating two-dollar chow mein after work every day as he stepped around the construction on Saint Laurent. People with money never went window shopping. And Damon would sure have liked to go to the Barfly, pick up some young thing and bang her from behind on a Monday night. He would do this last bit for revenge. He would wait until Ian was taking finals and then he would run through an economy size pack of condoms right up against the wall. Damon was desperate but he didn't think he was yet desperate enough to go along with Garry Hann.

Garry wanted to rob a med student. One of the kids who thought that a smile every now and again would be enough to keep them on Damon's good side. Little did they know...but rob them? That seemed a bit drastic. Garry seemed to have thought it through, though. He said it wasn't burglary but a class readjustment. He assured Damon that these young people were living off their parents who had made their fortunes off the backs of the hard-working man. Who was harder working than the Newfoundland man? That's what Garry wanted to know. Really, he said, it was like they were merely collecting what had been taken from their forefathers. Did Damon have access to home addresses? Did Damon know when they might have night classes? Yes, yes Damon did. The boys would pull themselves out of poverty, one Onterrible rich kid at a time. Hell, maybe they'd even be able to afford to fly home for a visit if there was a seat sale on.

Earlier in the term, Damon had developed an infatuation with a curly-haired girl who only rarely smiled at him, but who he'd seen talking to fucking Casanova. Ian seemed to be involved with all of his female classmates and the thought of him slipping down the panties of this particular girl made Damon want to vomit. It was his insane jealousy over this possibility that caused Damon to choose her as their first client. He would have preferred to rob young Ian next door, but figured it would be too obvious, make people on the street suspicious. Instead, Damon figured they could rob every girl spotted enjoying Ian's lame jokes. He decided that the girls would come to subconsciously suspect Ian was to be avoided and treat him like the plague. Hell, maybe they would somehow link Ian to the robberies. Damon could live with the idea of Ian serving time, paying for everything his social status had afforded him. Her name was Tiffany Wareham. Damon weaselled himself into the Registrar's office after hours and had a little poke through her files. She was an Anglo Montrealer which Garry deemed the worst kind.

Her family got enough money to ignore language. They could live in Bora Bora if they wanted to.

Tiffany was perfect. She lived on the ground floor, by herself, on the relatively quiet Rue Laval. She spent all of her free time at the library pouring over medical books while eating baby carrots on the sly. Garry determined that she was also a vegetarian.

It's funny, ain't it? The people who can afford proper meat then decides not to eat it.

The boys determined that the best day of the week to rob anyone was Thursday, the unofficial start of the weekend. They figured that by the time Ms. Wareham returned home that night it would be well into Friday morning. They thought that she wouldn't regain her composure until around mid-day Friday and that the police would certainly be head over heels chasing young black men around the Plateau for no apparent reason by the time Ms. Wareham was ready to discuss her case. And what was there to discuss, anyway? She barely spoke to Damon and even though she'd never seen Garry, they decided to go in disguise. They visited Value Village in preparation, bought tight girly jeans, old Converse sneakers and a couple of scarves. They bought medium-length curly brown wigs and stopped shaving. The boys were ready, in disguise, French hipsters. Brilliant. They'd be practically invisible. Slutty Marie had caught Garry at home the night they left to burgle the wannabe doctor so he was properly wound up when he reached Damon's house. Spitting curse words at her from across the provincial border and seething anxiety from every pore.

How do they decide those custody cases? I'd say it's who got the most cash for the lawyers' fees. Yes, we robs a few of those spoiled Toronto, those damn Toronto...after we robs them blind, I'm going to hire a lawyer and get the little fellow from that Marie, give him to Ma and go on vacation. Yes sir, fuck child support altogether. I'm going to get me money's worth. Yup, yup, in a couple hours I plan on fucking some girl who don't speak English. She don't have to speak French. I don't give a rat's ass what language she conducts her business in, as long as it's not English.

Garry had scouted out Tiffany's flat around the same time they had started growing their facial hair. He was confident going in through the back was the smartest idea, though he had never been involved in a criminal act of this magnitude before. Selling mushrooms on McMurdo's Lane was as big time as Garry had ever been, but he was more than willing to change this. Break and enter, he chanted until Damon told him to shut up, stop being an idiot. People didn't fucking croon B&E in the street. Garry tossed his grocery bag-covered fists through the first pane of Tiffany's bedroom window and then the second. For once, they were grateful for Montreal's shitty storm windows. Garry boosted Damon in to the bedroom and was quickly let in through the back door. Serves her right, he thought, for wanting "outdoor space." Yuppie.

No sooner inside than Damon became aware of the female smell that was missing from his life. He turned on the bedside lamp and scanned the room. A couple of mattresses lay on the floor neatly draped in homemade patchwork quilts. Beside the lamp lay a single amber ring and a photograph of Tiffany and an elderly woman. Old paperbacks lined the bureau, mostly plays and Russian literature. It wasn't the bedroom Damon expected. It was actually pretty stark.

She owns a wind-up clock.
The good stuff must be in the living room, Dame, b'y. Come on.

But there was no good stuff. A rust-coloured, second-hand sofa bed and grey litter box were the only pieces of furniture in the room alongside an oversized cherry desk, obviously the most expensive thing in the apartment. A *Metropolis* movie poster was the sole wall hanging, if you could call it that, being barely tacked to the wall. The room was full in its own way though, with stacks of books in every corner, papers piled neatly on both ends of the couch, anatomy textbooks lying spread eagle on the floor by the desk.

Where's the computer? Where's her god damn TV?
I guess she doesn't have one.
Who doesn't have a TV?
I don't.
Jesus! Jesus! Books. Look around for something valuable, something I can get rid of. Of all the fucking rich, fucking snotty bitches at that fucking school and you pick the one poor Misses.
Just shut it, Gar!
Fine, fucking fine. Abort, abort mission, I suppose.

So Garry and Damon couldn't even make it as petty criminals, leaving empty-handed, all ambition for a career in robbery blasted. Truth be told, Garry was so dejected by the whole experience that he called Slutty Marie—collect—and had a cry. He begged her not to keep the young fellow from his mother, and when that didn't work he started saying nice stuff to her about her vagina being tight and whatever. Before Gar knew what was going on, he was having full on phone sex with his baby mama. He felt dirty when it was over and was certain ol' Marie would figure some way to get herself knocked up. That woman was after him.

Damon was glad the whole thing fell apart: shitting in the street is one thing, actually breaking the law is something else altogether. And sure, Damon couldn't steal from someone who had less than him. Yeah, he was feeling that everything had been for the best until he arrived at work the next day to find the med school covered in missing cat posters. Jesus. Find Rufus posters. Damon hadn't meant for the damn cat to get out. That wasn't his intention. And the curly-haired one was all puffy-eyed and weepy when she came to collect her tibula. Damon couldn't look at the sorry state of the blonde he'd been wanking it to for months. He felt something akin to guilt...and opportunity.

Garry, we got to go find that girl's cat.
Yes, b'y. That's just what I wants to go at. Spends all day looking at cat arse, now I'm going searching for cat arse all night. You're cracked.

We lost her cat.

Whatever, cats get lost all the damn time. And besides, I'm busy.

Doing what?

Packing.

Packing?

Yup, throwing it in.

Going home to your mother, are you?

Something like that.

Garry Hann was the useless sack Damon always knew him to be. Damon swore to not waste another single minute associated with the Hanns. Sure, what good did it do him? This was what he thought about as he searched the back alleys of the Plateau calling for some cat named Rufus. Here he was a decent enough guy, a handsome guy, smart too, a catch really, definitely better than that Brenda Hann. Here he was now practically a derelict, out in the dark, stinking of tuna, meowing his heart out after this cat he's only seen on a poster. A cat that he was after losing cause he let buddy b'y talk him into smashing out that poor Misses's windows. But things were going to change. Oh yes, Damon had a new plan that included getting out of his shit apartment and banging a doctor for the rest of his days. Damon had decided his goal in life.

Hello.

Ah, hi. I think I found your cat.

Oh my god, oh Rufus. Oh thank you, thank you.

It was nothing.

No, really. Thank you. He's like the only friend I have in the world. Oh Rufus Smufus, where were you?

Well...ah, see ya around, guess.

Hey, don't I know you from school?

Yeah, I work there.

Oh, wow. What are the chances of that hey?

I know. Weird.

Let Garry Hann go off home a failure, end up shacked up with

Slutty Marie and his special youngster. Let Brenda go off to Alberta. Damon hopes she ends up on the corner somewhere, street meat for rig pigs. Yes sir, the hell with Newfoundland and everybody stuck on it. The weather is the shits anyhow. Damon was going get his and now he knew where.

I don't know how to thank you. Really, I mean...would you like to come in? Would you like, I don't know...a beer or something?

Yeah, yeah actually...I would. I think I would love a beer.

ENTHUSIASTIC
ABOUT POTATOES

I am the blackest man working at Tim Hortons. There are other black men, but I am the blackest. There are also Canadian women. Students. But they work to get maternity leave or to gain access to the university parking lot. One shift a week earns them a parking permit. They all have cars. These girls who go to university. They have their own cars. They do not have to share. One pretty blonde girl does, but it's with her older sister. They live together in a house bought by their parents. She complains about this endlessly. It's a huge inconvenience. I write my brother in Nigeria. I tell him that everyone has more than they need here and yet, they are starving.

Every second day, the same woman buys an iced cappuccino with a shot of mint. She does a class called shallow-water fitness at lunch. This class is mostly for elderly women and fat babes. She belongs to the latter group. I hope the woman's name is Peggy or Margery. I like soft women with soft names. I make plans to ask her. I will give her an Iced Cap on the house, a large one with two shots of mint. I will attend shallow-water fitness. I will take her to the Wal-Mart.

I will never do any of these things.

Because I don't have to. One day she speaks to me. She asks me where I am from. Not my name but where I am from. Then what I am doing here. Then how old I am. Then if I drink. I think that names must not be important here. I am disappointed that her name is Pamela. She says everyone calls her Pam except her father. He calls her Pammy. Pammy. I try to tell her my name but she already knows. She asked the girl who shares a car.

She buys us tater poutines from Mary Brown's and we eat them in a parking lot across from a high school. She cannot wait. She says she is famished and then apologizes because she has seen little kids without pants covered in flies on the television. I tell her that it was not like that for me even though it was. Instead, I tell her that my family is well off and I am only working at the Tim's until I start university in the fall. I tell her there has been a mistake with my transcripts, an international, bureaucratic mistake. Newfoundlanders seem to prefer reams of excuses to the truth, so I elaborate. I actually did very well in school, was third in my class, and ran competitively. These lies put her at ease and she fishes up the last string of orange cheese with her white plastic fork.

I hates plastic cutlery, she says. It's right flimsy.

Her father has fed her fine. She is enthusiastic about potatoes. I wonder if she can debone a chicken. The girls I work with don't know how to do anything. Yet, they are full of pride. The girl who shares the car says she will be like her older sister who married a chef. She says visiting her sister is like going to a fine dining restaurant for free. I think, someone must pay for that food. That same girl spends hours decorating gourmet cupcakes but never eats one. Everything tasted better at home, like food grown from the earth. Food tastes vague here, less than the version of itself I knew in Nigeria. Weaker. I miss pounded vegetable stew. I miss it especially when I eat boiled dinner. Newfoundlanders appreciate salt meat, too. I am sometimes homesick on Sundays.

Pam loves bite-sized brownies. I watch her eat four or five unconsciously, as she swerves her car through traffic. Pam has started to drive me places. She says it's not safe to walk. She is a confident driver. She can eat peanuts and shift at the same time. Her dad taught her to drive in an extended cab pick-up truck, she says. Now, she can park anything anywhere. Except downtown. But she doesn't go downtown often.

I hates it down there, she says. All the girls is right slutty.

We go to the cinema and she buys a nachos and a diet soda. I buy a pack of candy and offer them to her. Her eyes light up with every red strip and she chews for a long time. Longer than is necessary. Concentrated. After the film, she confesses that it's really great that I drink. She acts as if alcohol was invented here. I don't correct her. I like that she wants me to fit in. All of Pam's rooms are fattening rooms. She says she has always been a big girl and I'm certain people will think I am rich. She has the correct living particulars.

She tells me she has diabetes; that it's in her family. Her great-grandmother had both legs amputated from the knees down. They called her Granny Stubs because she was unfriendly. Granny Stubs was part native. I ask which part and Pam accidentally blows Diet Orange Crush out her nose.

She says, she has never been with anyone like me. That she hasn't been with many men. She was afraid of sex. Once she had sex with her brother's friend and now he likes men. And women. I was afraid of sex all the time at home, I say, but I am not afraid anymore. She does not even make me use a rubber. I tell the guys in the kitchen where I work my second job and they laugh and call me *crazy man*. I continue washing up. I have no idea what is crazy about making love with your girlfriend. The guys in the kitchen don't have girlfriends. The owner doesn't have a girlfriend. They are older than I am and not interested in women. They prefer to watch each other scream into microphones. They do this in dark bars with water-damaged ceilings and holes in the walls. The only women that attend date

27

members of the band or want to. I think, maybe they are the crazy ones.

I know I am Pam's boyfriend because I have met her father. We drove out to his village in her car on skinny, slippery roads while animals hid in the trees. This man owns three leather sofas and a large television that is kept on all day, every day. He says it's to keep his wife company. His mother, who lives with them, does a poor job of this. The elderly Mrs. O'Keefe tells me repeatedly that I am some dark. She whispers after dinner that there was rumour of a brown baby in her family after the war. But no one knows what happened there. I smile and watch Pam sip her light beer. Later, her father says he is glad Pammy got a man. They were worried she'd be alone forever like her Aunt Jose.

Aunt Jose is a very large woman. She does not get around well, complains of the wood stove and picks the dirt under her fingernails. People have to come to her. She becomes sulky and childish if they do not spend enough time sitting, chatting beside her. She orders her groceries to be delivered to her house because she no longer drives her car. She used to drive her car, but she had a little accident and could not get out. Not because she was injured. Just because. They had to get the jaws of life to remove her. Aunt Jose does not look like the woman in Pam's family pictures. Thirty years ago, Aunt Jose had beautiful calves.

Pam is having a baby! I am so happy. I am practically Canadian. I want us to get married, but she says she wants to drink at our wedding. So we must wait. I take additional shifts in the kitchen. Everyone buys my baby diapers. Pam spends hours every day reading mommy blogs. Sometimes, when she is bored of this, she switches to wedding blogs. She is tremendously stressed for a woman on Employment Insurance. Pam's father owns boats. He is buying us a house in a town called Paradise. This Paradise has no trees; it's all roads and houses. Pam bristles when I mention how far away it is from my jobs. She says something about dirty dishwater and does not even say thank you when I bring her home Timbits. I have never had a bedroom this big before. There is a dishwasher in the kitchen that makes no noise.

My bruv calls. Our cousin's application has been successful

and he is coming to Canada. I feel like my whole life is starting. I cannot wait to tell Pam. I call her cellphone which she answers even though she is driving. I explain about my cousin and living with us in Paradise. Pam says, no, like it's her decision. When I object, she says it's her house. Her house. Then she says I have to learn to worry about my own people. This confuses me. My cousin is my own people.

And Pammy says, not any more Wale.

A SINK BUILT FOR SMALLER PEOPLE

Mom warns that I will be overcome with remorse the moment the plane takes off, but I'm not. Not when we ascend in St. John's, Halifax or even Toronto. All I feel is urgency—get me away from here, farther away, now even farther, farther still. Until finally we land in Seoul and I feel a William Wallace level of triumph. Only instead of a vocal explosion, I whisper *freedom* to myself while Bruce is in the bathroom. We are exhausted, wrinkled puppies looking for our owner. But we're happy. And excited. The flight is fine, long but uneventful. I watch a tiny plane depict where we hang in the sky and think of how it seems to pull our flight along. I have never flown over an ocean before. I'm not scared, not really. Neither are the Filipino babies in our section who are content to suckle for the better part of fifteen hours. Twice they serve miso soup and I feel I will suddenly explode with worldliness. I read two reasonably sized novels and our travel guide while Bruce sleeps. He can sleep anywhere. It's like his superpower. That and being right. Bruce is correct in most things. He is as correct as Mom is incorrect...usually. The school's janitor picks us up because of the early hour. He has our names written poorly on a piece of printer paper in case there are other white people on our flight. There aren't. Seeing our names: a sudden jolt. Bruce! Ellen! The drive to our apartment—or Asian sleeping closet as it would later be known—is littered with lit red and green crosses sitting upon rooftops. I worry a little about religion.

Our apartment is not what was described over the phone, but we are in no position to argue, which works quite well for Korean recruitment officers. There are mattresses on the floor facing a television, there is a stovetop and a mini-fridge. Here is what there isn't. There is no oven, there are no pillows, no blankets, no towels, no household items of any kind. Not even a glass to drink bottled water from. There is no bottled water. The janitor tells us not to drink the tap water and I am suddenly aware of my thirst. I am so fucking thirsty. Take rest, he says, pointing to the bare mattress, and then leaves. We do, Bruce does. The next morning I feel wired, deluded in my exhaustion and crazed with thirst. But I don't wake him. Bruce and I have been together a year and a half, long enough to know better. He sleeps corpse-like, hands folded across his chest, a towel that I demanded we bring covering his right leg. I also brought framed photos and four books. I am watching the firemen across the street wash their truck and think they are the most Asians I have ever seen in one place. I am regarding the pads of Bruce's feet. The white and pink lines within the arch slowly morphing into orange toward his heels, yellow where they support his body weight. I decide I cannot wait for him to wake and leave in search of water and food.

Outside I am instantly a fat girl. I have never been a fat girl before. I am a bull in a china shop, I am sweat and blotches, I am all breasts and hips. I think again, that there are a lot of Asians here. I try to adapt quickly, I shade my face, I take in landmarks. Around the corner I find a bakery. I buy bread and cheese, bottled water and apples. I am surprised by how similar transactions occur on both sides of the world, and I hurry back to our apartment before I get a sunburn. This is a very hot sun for so early in the morning. I worry a little, but not a lot. I'll figure it out. We'll figure it out. Bruce is sleeping as soundly as he would at home in his parents' basement and I remind myself that travelling is old hat for my lovely, lean boyfriend. I wash an apple with a little bottled water, sparing it as best I can, standing next to a sink built for smaller people. I think about what it will be like to not have a bathtub for an entire year. When Bruce wakes we eat the bread and cheese and wonder if anyone from the school will come for us. I toast the bread over an open flame using a metal hanger I found in a closet—twelve years of Girl Guides finally paying off in this one moment of resourcefulness. The bread is oddly sweet, causing breakfast to feel desert-like. Appropriate in a way, Bruce muses, considering we are on the other side of the world. He jokes about going down the rabbit hole and we take a shower together, drying each other off with our one towel.

The story of the towel: Bruce had very strong feelings concerning what I packed and did not pack to move to Korea. I would not need warmer formal clothing, he said. I could buy it there. I would not need a towel or bedding, he said. They would be provided. Books could always be gotten and framed photos were just ludicrous. He was right about the framed photos.

We dress in T-shirts and shorts due to the heat. Bruce investigates what looks to be a air conditioner until our boss arrives. Tony Kim once lived in British Columbia for three months and therefore feels very knowledgeable concerning the Newfoundlanders he has hired to teach English. Tony Kim does not know how to hide disapproval: it spreads across his face like a bad smell. Our shorts aren't appropriate attire for school, and my accent is puzzling. Bruce explains that we were unaware we were expected at school this morning. Tony Kim retorts that we were hired to be teachers, not tourists. I convince myself his tone and expectations are a result of some misunderstanding and my own exhaustion.

The school is three floors of a rundown office tower. The halls are grimy and dark. The only light throughout is florescent, shades on the windows are required to keep the scorching sunshine out. Children of all ages crowd us as we tour the class-rooms, whispering and pulling on my green skirt. They reach for the hair on Bruce's arms, stroking it and giggling *monkey teacher*. I am handed a book and left in a classroom to teach English. I watch Bruce and Tony Kim walk toward the teachers' lounge. Tony Kim is looking forward to introducing us to the other ESL teacher, though I will have to wait until after class. The group of twelve-year-old students are really eleven because Koreans start counting from one at birth. Also, I am told that eight months is the average duration of pregnancy, and that their national dish, a fermented cabbage called kimchi, is the cure for cancer. One extremely brave boy asks if maybe I am having a baby because my breasts are so large. Like a pregnant woman's, he says.

Don, the other teacher, is American. He's from Colorado or Las Vegas or Minnesota. He tells Koreans he is Ricky from Toronto though he has never been to Canada. He tells us he does this for safety. The president is not popular in Seoul. He is unpopular, so unpopular in fact that even the children ask if you like *Bushy*. I can sincerely say I don't and am thankful for this. Lying has become a constant and unavoidable part of surviving in our new home. Bruce and I have become liars. Don has been at our school for three years but is planning a move to Taiwan in two months. We barely adjust to the odd thirty-year-old's deceptions before we are celebrating his departure. He gets very drunk for someone who claims not to drink. But everyone gets very drunk in Korea.

My awareness of my massive body has developed into an eating disorder. This is in part a result of not being able to buy clothing of any kind. Shop girls rush me out of clothing stores adamant that they have no *big sizes* for me. They do this repeatedly and in front of Bruce. I was a size six in Canada. I call Mom and ask her to send me dress pants in the mail. Winter is coming and I'll be needing pants, I say. My new infatuation with anorexia is also in part due to Bruce's new interest in learning

34

Korean from a young Korean English teacher at our school. At lunch they sit cross-legged on the floor, shoulders touching, while they eat hearty servings of fish and rice. I sit across from them and slowly eat whatever vegetables are being served that day. I suffer through large portions of kimchi because I am so hungry. The Korean cook loves that I eat so much kimchi, and I become her new favourite based on this alone. I have sworn off rice until I am able to find pants that fit or Bruce starts paying attention to me again. Da-Som teaches him the Korean alphabet and I go skip on the roof in the searing afternoon sun. When we drink I become deliriously drunk on rice wine and end up being dragged home by an angry Bruce. I bawl myself to sleep on the floor but tell Pop things are awesome when he calls in the morning. Pop is worried sick about me living in Asia—he has bad nerves. But he is also astounded by the clarity of the telephone connection and calls often because of this. You could be next door sure, Ellen, he says, and I think this is too much for my twenty-one years to navigate. The whole undertaking is ridiculous.

I become obsessed with saving my money so I never have to go back to Korea ever again. Bruce is the opposite. He doesn't have a student loan; he wants to go to China. He wants to backpack around Southeast Asia and spend time in Japan. I want to go home, but I don't say that because we have so many months left that it makes me crazy to think about it. In fact, I pretend that I live in Korea. That Seoul is my home, always has been and always will be. We all do. All us twenty-something ESL teachers from across the English-speaking world pretend we belong where we are. We try to one-up each other with how much we belong. We gleefully gossip about some Brit or Yank who pulled a runner in the middle of the night all the way home because they couldn't handle it. They weren't cut out for it. This happens all the time and it makes us feel like we are winning. We don't know what we're winning, but we are all aware of the competition we unknowingly entered into. There are many categories, some overlapping: happiest couple, most money saved, most countries visited, best job, best apartment, etc. The competitive spirit of the grossly overpopulated Asian capital has infected us and we are practically hateful to one another.

Don's replacement finally arrives. Her name is Jaclyn and she is from Australia. She has already been teaching all over Asia even though she doesn't have a degree. She claims to have received her education from *The World*; experience is her university. Bruce admires this. I try hard to. I am desperate for female contact; I will hang out with any girl who speaks English. ESL teaching is predominately for guys: they are worshipped in Asia, they are prizes—the wildly-coveted, foreign boyfriend. The only men who ever hit on me are other homesick Canadians—Newfoundlanders especially love me. My accent reminds them of their mothers. But I don't want to talk to men anymore, I am tired of talking to men...Bruce. Bruce loves Asia. He wants us to sign on for another year. The thought of this incites expensive late-night phone calls to my girlfriends. I leave slurring messages on answering machines all over St. John's. I attempt to woo Jaclyn with trips to Wal-Mart; I show her where to buy French baguettes and proper cheese. But she wants nothing to do with me.

Instead she tells Bruce how she doesn't want the things normal women want: doesn't want a house or a car, doesn't believe in marriage—that outdated institution. She says she doesn't want kids. She knows all this at twenty-five, so she says. Bruce happily swallows this down whole, as if it's the most delicious information he has ever tasted. But I know right away what she is up to; I'm a woman, I have played that game before. We all have. And I begin to hate Jacklyn for what she really is: the woman who is trying to steal my boyfriend. I realize I could have never liked her anyway—this blonde airhead; this vapid nomad. Jacklyn is a woman meant to soak in sunshine; she doesn't require frequent applications of sunblock. She doesn't even sweat. She is tiny and has never been in love. All of her Facebook profile pictures are taken from above in that intentional sexy manner. I fucking loathe her. I imagine her being eaten by a shark, but smile at her from across our shared worktable. Bruce is no longer interested in learning Korean.

We only have three weeks left of our contract and I am in a hurry to give away all of our worldly possessions. I want to be done with our cheap forks and spoons, I want to cleanse the Asian sleeping closet of Ellen and Bruce. I want us to go back to before. I want to rewind. Bruce is not so impatient to rid himself of our things, to bequeath our worldly possessions to another Newfoundland couple that has recently arrived. I am so full of forewarning that I scare the young woman half to death. Ten days before our flight Bruce informs me he doesn't want to go back to North America, maybe ever. That he has no direction there, he has nothing to go West for. A monumental screaming match ensues. I accuse him of avoidance, fantasies of grandeur and the like. We don't even fuck before I leave. All I feel when I board my flight is that same urgency—get me away from here, farther away, now even farther, farther still. But Mom is right. I am full of remorse, it pours out of my face uncontrollably. I fill packs of tissues with it; the mothers in my section are certain there has been a death. And there has. A month later, Facebook tells me Bruce is travelling in Australia. I'm not surprised. He could always sleep anywhere.

HOUSEPLANTS
AND PICTURE FRAMES

Your father doesn't care about you Sadie, Mom says. He never thinks about you at all. He hardly knows you're in the world.

And I worry no one will ever care about me, or think about me, or know I'm in the world, if my own father doesn't. But I don't say this because Mom is on a roll. It's Saturday afternoon and she's still in her pajamas. She has been up since seven; she has mixed a bread, washed the floors, started the laundry, fed everyone, twice, and cleaned the litter box. Dad is still in bed. Last night he went to a meeting over at the Lions Club and now he's really tired. Dad is always really tired after he goes to meetings. I'm supposed to go to cross-country skiing in forty-five minutes. They call it Jackrabbits but rabbits don't ski. Mom says she can't drive me to Jackrabbits because Damey has a head cold and shouldn't be dragged out into February just because my father is useless.

Mom says that if it wasn't for her, we'd live in a cardboard box. She says there wouldn't be a lick of paint on the walls! And what paint there was, would be the cheapest you could buy any-where in the world. The kind of paint that would make every stick of furniture look shabby. The kind of paint that would make everyone who saw it, think you were doing poorly. White paint. Or light green, like at Nan's. Your father, she says, wouldn't notice though. Because he doesn't notice a thing. And then Mom discovers a new leak in the laundry room over the yellow ironing board that has green apples on it. She's running off down the hallway muttering about all that snow built up on the roof. All that Jesus snow. I know this is big time stuff because Mom only uses the J-word when it's big time stuff.

Your father don't give a Jesus about anything as long as he got cigarettes and enough money to get drunk at the bar.

And I know this is kind of true. I wish it wasn't, but I know it is because Dad has spent his last ten dollars on smokes before when there was no milk in the fridge. Keeping milk in the fridge is one of Mom's jobs. Mom has got a lot of jobs. She washes all the dirty stuff. And remembers to buy all the birthday presents. Mom pays the bills out of her money that she makes being the principal of my school. Dad's money is for the truck. And boat. And bike. Dad's money is for transportation. He says that he used to have a lot more money before Mom came along and spent it all on clothes. He says this all the time. That, and how he paid for her teaching diploma. Mom's eyes get right big when he mentions her teaching diploma. Mom says she didn't know that Dad was buying into every cent she made for the rest of her life. She says he's been paid back a million times over. And then they get loud.

I go in the bedroom to make sure Damey doesn't get scared. He's little so he doesn't understand that our Mom and Dad are wild. That's what the woman at the drugstore said. She asked me if dad still lived in the house and when I said he never, she said it was a sin that my mom and dad was right wild. Dad was living in our camper in the yard then. He used to come in the house while Mom was at school. He would shower and eat all of his food for the day from nine to four-thirty. He didn't take any of the nice clothes Mom bought him either. He only took his stereo. Dad loves music. He has a wonderful singing voice. And he is really creative. People like him a lot. He can make anyone laugh, just like that. Cool dads are always in trouble with moms. And my dad has a motorcycle, so, you know, he sleeps in the camper a lot. Mom says that next time she is going to marry a nice, boring man with a nice, boring job. No one like my father, she tells me. Nothing like your father.

Dad was sleeping in the camper that time because he sent back Mom's new couch. Sears called and said that our parcel had arrived. It was over twelve hundred dollars C.O.D so Dad went to Sears on his bike to find out what it was. Dad said he couldn't believe it when he saw it was a goddamn couch. He said he was right embarrassed because it was obvious his wife orders big purchases without his permission. Mom hates the word "permission" at home. She loves it at school. But she hates it at home. When Dad says permission, Mom starts to spit and wave her arms around. Damey cries because she looks wild so I take him into the playroom and let him play with my Barbies. This is a special treat. Usually he isn't allowed to play with my Barbies because he pulls their heads off in his mouth.

Mom says she doesn't need permission. And Dad says to just imagine, just imagine, if he had ordered a new couch without Mom's input. He says she could have at least asked his opinion. Mom says Dad can start having an opinion when he starts paying for stuff. Then Dad says there's nothing wrong with the couch we have. And Mom is threatening to set that Jesus hand-me-down couch on fire again. The first time she said that, I got really worried because I didn't know where my cat was. Peaches gets stuck in closets all the time because he goes in there to rub himself all over Mom's black dress pants and someone always shuts the door on him by accident. I thought he would die in the fire, so I came up with a fire drill plan like on the *Kindergarten Cop* movie. That was before Damey. Sometimes now, I worry that I won't be able to get Damey and Peaches out if Mom burns the couch. They don't like each other. Peaches doesn't like Damey because babies are rude to cats. But Mom hasn't done it yet and she says she will all the time, so I don't think she's going to.

Dad always brings up a lawnmower he paid for when Mom says he doesn't pay for stuff. We don't have that lawnmower any-more, but Dad reminds everyone that he paid for it. It was some-thing Mom wanted and didn't have any money for. He got it for her as a big surprise. Mom says some surprise, she knows. The big surprise was that Dad never used it; would watch Mom mow the lawn when she was pregnant, both times. That's the kind of man my father is. The kind of man who hauls all the beautiful tulip bulbs from the ground rather than seal up the holes in the foundation. Dad thinks tulip bulbs and birdseed are mouse food. He says that's why there are always little mice droppings on the cutting board. But Mom says there's mouse poop on the cutting board because Dad didn't pour enough foundation, that hauling her tulip bulbs out of the Jesus ground is deference. She says that he is only pretending to deal with the problem. Mom says Dad focuses his attentions on cosmetic issues rather than deal with actual issues. Like when we have a New Year's Eve party, Dad spends all evening moving the houseplants and picture frames around while Mom cleans the bathroom and the kitchen. Mom says that if there was a dying man with his leg hanging off and a broken toe, Dad would fix the broken toe while Mom saved the man's leg and then pretend they did the same amount of work. Pretend he did more work, expect praise. Mom says Dad's prior-ities boggle her Jesus mind.

Sometimes I think my head will explode because of Mom and Dad.

Like when Mom went away to a teachers' conference in Gan-der; Dad had a wood stove put in the house to save money on the sly. Mom got wild when she came home because she thinks this is typical of Dad. She says he is doing it half-assed and that we do not live back in the olden days. Spending less money is not the same as making more money, doesn't he know that? She says she is really going to divorce him this time. I go for walks when Mom uses the D-word. I go for walks in the woods and make up stories about having a different life. Sometimes in my stories, I am a princess. But most of the time, I am just a little girl with a tame Mom and Dad. And a quiet house. And a dog instead of a cat.

Dad wanted to be in a Newfoundland band. He wanted to travel up and down the coast playing jigs and reels about fishing. Mom says she was supportive of this, she tells me all the time how she supported Dad. He played at graduations and berry festivals. He was really popular. Mom booked these gigs for years; she was a teacher and Dad's manager. See, my Mom has a lot of jobs. Then she had me and she didn't have time to manage Dad anymore. Mom says, he can go on and play music all he likes, she'd love it if he made more money. But Dad doesn't have the first clue about bookings because he never took any interest into it. Dad isn't a go-getter, she says. Dad thinks everything is just supposed to work out for him. Like magic. Mom says that's Nan's fault and I don't like that very much because I think Nan is a saint. She will give you jam crackers before supper and let you play with her false teeth. Nan has got a good sense of humour. She is interested in whatever you are interested in. Nan will let you stay up and watch *90210* even when Mom tells her that it's not age appropriate. Nan doesn't want you to be the only one on the bus that never saw it. Nan understands.

Mom says Dad doesn't take interest in me and Damey but that's not true. Sometimes, he does. And those are the best times. Sometimes Dad takes me ice fishing, just us, and we celebrate when I jig a trout up by the tail. And sometimes Dad plays board games with me and teaches me how to be a better banker. Dad makes math more interesting than Mom. And I don't mind playing boy games, if Dad likes playing boy games because it makes him in a good mood. And everyone likes Dad better when he's in a good mood. Sometimes that makes Mom sad but most of the time, she is okay with it because she is too busy vacuuming the carpet to be fun anyway. Mom likes to keep straight lines in the carpet in case any of her relatives come visit. This proves she's a good mom.

Mom says that I wouldn't know how to do anything if she left it up to Dad. I wouldn't know how to dribble, or skate, or ride bike. Mom says she made Dad teach me all of those things; that some moms don't make dads do that and then the kids don't know how to do anything when they're all grown up. I wish Mom would not tell me stuff that makes me feel bad. Because I was feeling good about Dad teaching me how to carry a puck until Mom said she made him. It's not the same now. Sometimes I get mad at Mom when she is yelling at Dad to do stuff. I say, why don't you just do it! It would be easier. And Mom asks easier for who? Who would it be easier for Sadie? And then she is mad at me.

I never know which team I want to be on. I wish I could be on both teams but Mom and Dad are only on the same team when they are playing against Uncle Bill or Aunt Charlotte. Uncle Bill is Dad's older brother and Aunt Charlotte is Mom's older sister. Mom and Dad get really wild with them. There are never enough lines in the carpet for Aunt Charlotte. Sometimes she comes over when no one is home and vacuums. This makes Dad crazy, but I know Aunt Charlotte is just trying to older-sister-help because I'm an older sister, too. I worry that Damey will not like me when he gets big so I am even nicer to him. Even nicer than I want to be. I do everything for him I can think so he will like me later.

The worse thing you can be at our house is *just like* someone. Like when Dad is mad, I am just like my mother. And when Mom is mad, I am just like my father. I am never like both of them at the same time. Someone is always angry and yelling at half of me. I get used to this. I practice everything really hard. I write my letters for hours at the table until they are perfect letters. I colour pictures in my book for hours until they are perfect pictures. I show Mom and Dad all the good things I can do so that they will like all the parts of me. I take care of Damey so they won't fight. I do really good on my tests so they can brag.

But they don't brag, not really. Only when I get a hundred. When I get less than a hundred, they always ask about the other points. Like when I get ninety-six, Dad asks where the other four points went? There is room for improvement. I can always be better.

You can do better, Sadie.

I WILL HATE
EVERYTHING, LATER

B thinks a week on the beach will make up for the life he's given me. What an idiot. As if a week of warm sunshine and weak cocktails could erase three years of oppression. I am oppressed. The constant squabbling, the verbal abuse, the sexual harassment. I never wanted any of this. I spent my whole young life fleeing it. Now, I spend my Saturdays at birthday parties trying to make small talk with boring women while Jack is temporarily distracted by the other children. Jack is the very reason we are in Cuba. We have vacated him, 'cause that's what a vacation is; an opportunity to vacate our child. B doesn't see it that way because he spends all his time at the restaurant. His mornings are full of streaming radio, flavoured coffee and solitude. The first hour he spends in the kitchen alone before the staff start to trickle in at ten. The lovely young waitresses he hires for their personalities. As if. B tells people that we go on vacation to *reconnect*. He hates it when I tell the truth. That Jack assaulted me. That I threatened to leave.

B says Jack did not assault me. That three-year olds don't assault their mothers, but B wasn't there. He never is. And Jack is a little pervert. Like his father. He is always sporting tiny boners. It's gross. He refuses to acknowledge my boundaries. He acts like my body is just another thing to ruin. I should have never breast-fed. I love him. I love him to pieces. I just don't like him. I don't like my son. B was aghast the first time I said it. He blamed it on the weather. The rain made me say it. The fog was affecting me. It happens. In Newfoundland. Newfoundland. What a horrible banal name. It's painfully appropriate. I hate my fucking life.

The line for our flight was full of young men with awful facial hair, heavy couples, and children. Other people's children. I remark that B had better have booked us into an adults-only resort and he does not respond. This, I know, means I will have to endure the theatrics of some stranger's brat on holiday. My god, this man, how did I end up with this man? Why on earth did I marry him? I don't even believe in marriage. There were so many other possibilities. Sri in India. Takashi in Japan. Hans, Vadim, Stewart, Alistar, Paulo. My God, Paulo. Instead, I choose Bruce. I will never comprehend my atrocious decision-making powers. I am epic in my self-deception. I call him B as a reproach. And Jack. After myself. As if to bind us together. I am a great riddle. A ridiculous prank. All self-inflicted.

B and I cannot sit together on the flight because he bought the bargain holiday on some sell-off website. He sits four rows ahead of me and looks back at me with expectation as the plane descends. That eager grin spreading across his face. Everyone claps when we land. They are so grateful. These peasants. And I think, *Jesus.*

The warm air feels familiar. I am of this air. I am a hot exotic living a cold existence. I remember a news article about elephants in Canadian zoos. How ill-suited they were for the temperatures. Bob Barker claiming it was inhumane to keep them in Edmonton. I think Corner Brook is inhumane, and decide I am never going back. B's fat sister will raise Jack with her perfect, caramel children. Pamela will feed him Kraft Dinner and let him drink soda in the morning. I imagine my Jack with rotten teeth and vow to never let this happen. There is something wrong with that family. Something curious about wanting to be of another place while remaining exactly where you are and have always been. B tricked me. He's just like them.

I know nothing about the resort. I didn't want to know. I left it all to Prince Charming so that I might hate it all later. Cayo Coco. I can despise anything. It's a gift. B is thrilled with the place. He wears a straw hat and goes on about swimming in the ocean. I remind him that he has been to far more exciting places and he gives me a wounded look. Jack has made him sensitive. I preferred him before. Cocksure and unapologetic. Now he wants a quad. And a daughter. He says he would like one of each, a boy and a girl, as if they were different flavours of milk you pull from the market fridge. I try to imagine two screaming children climbing me. I try to be okay with the image. I am not. In front of us stands a trio of women with a child Jack's age. A girl. She is lovely and quiet and clean. She is pulling a small, pink suitcase behind her like a miniature globetrotter. I think of Jack this morning. Oatmeal in his nose. Dunking my cellphone in his orange juice. These are the funniest things in the whole world. Filling holes with goo and breaking Mommy's things. I definitely don't want another one. I don't know if I want the one I have. In front of the trio of women are two other couples. The men barely speak. The women never stop speaking.

We pass hundreds of cows on our way to the resort. They aren't native to Cuba. An American farmer abandoned them here decades ago. Now, they are flourishing. B exclaims, just like moose at home! Right. Home. Pfft. I remember picking broccoli as a teenager and my father drinking lager on the porch. Now I pick berries on the side of a cliff and shovel my way in and out of a basement apartment. B's father has offered to help us, but that man of mine insists it will become an infringement on our freedom. I remark that I have no freedom, that I would happily sacrifice *his* freedom for an above-ground entrance and a second bathroom with a lock. He says we would have to move to the other side of the island away from the mountain. And I shriek, what mountain? I haven't been boarding in over three fucking years. He retorts that we went at least a half-dozen times last season. But that doesn't count. We had Jack and we can never have fun with Jack. He will not allow it. He is insanely jealous of anything Mommy might enjoy better than him. It's impossible. And wonderful. I am ashamed of myself for my divided heart. I spent my whole pregnancy lying. You must be excited, they would squeal. Oh yeah, I'm excited, I would lie as Jack used my ribcage to leverage himself, stringing my ribs with his foot like a toy guitar stored there for his own amusement.

The quiet men and their loud partners decide to set up next to us on the beach. We have the best spot. They invade our personal space because they have no clue concerning beach etiquette. Or they don't care. They probably don't care. I've met hundreds of Newfoundlanders like that. Mistaking despicable manners for hospitality. No doubt in the past, this legendary friendliness existed on B's island, but it doesn't anymore. The two women walk into the ocean together talking loudly. Their voices bounce back over the sea, offensive sound waves of poor grammar. They squat just as the water reaches their knees and urinate across from each other with their arms resting on their legs. The conversation about nothing never ceases as pee streams from their bikini bottoms. B strikes up a friendship with the men. They were born in the same hospital. This is enough apparently. Less would have likely sufficed with this bunch. Later that night, after we manage to get drunk, I complain that the women do not like me. I say "we" because B and I are the only couple to get properly drunk and I say "manage" because it's a challenge with the little plastic glasses holding the tiniest splash of rum. B doesn't understand why I care. He says I would never speak to those women at home. He suggests that maybe they can sense this, that I am some kind of snob. I demand that he shut up with his nonsense. And then I demand that he walk to the lounge and get me a grilled ham sandwich. I am starving. There is a lot of food on offer in the buffet, at least by Cuban standards. B gorges himself on oily cheese and seafood everyday. He loves buffets. But I am so hungry...every minute of the day I think about food. What I will eat next. Should I eat now or after the next chapter in the Tom Robbins' novel I am reading? Now or after I snorkel around the reef with the Belarussian couple I have befriended. Now or after B and I retire to our room for mid-day sex, shampoo and BBC updates. When will I eat? It consumes me.

We sit with the trio of women and the globetrotting toddler on our second-last day. All of the buffet tables are full and our server, who specializes in Newfoundland history, insists we will like these people. Each server specializes in a province to impress on the Canadians how interesting and relevant Canada is. They do so, of course, for money, which seems to bother no one. I again declare that I am not from Newfoundland or Canada but no one hears me or cares. The family is from northern Ontario. They happily argue with B over who has it worse. They do so completely without irony, as if competing for lousiest life were entirely natural. Though, the youngest is a doll. So tidy and po-lite. She obeys her Aunt Clare and grandmother as easily as she does her mother. She does not cling or climb or bite or hit. She spills nothing on herself during dinner and eats things Jack would never consider food. I am in love with her. I do not want Jack to be like her: I want Jack to be her.

They discuss returning to winter while I consider kidnapping.

A week isn't long enough, two weeks is too long. Blah blah blah. They are predictable in their small talk, B and these women who all resemble each other to the point of annoyance. Thank goodness B looks nothing like his family. Or I don't think he does. Either way, I'm annoyed by these women and their per-fect heir, who, without provocation or bribery, sinks down into her chair to sleep. Just effortlessly naps in her chair while her grandmother, mother and aunt continue drinking wine to drunkenness. I'm also drunk. Though I'm as irritated as they are relaxed. I make a snide comment about potentially losing my passport on purpose after becoming suspicious of B. Is he flirting with these women? The aunt snaps that this is a stupid, fucking joke and our table grows quiet. The pin drops. She blushes and explains she lost her passport once in Thailand. That it was stolen. She was very afraid and alone, not knowing what would happen. Her sister reaches for her hand, the doll wakes and the trio of women retire to their room with their secrets intact.

The next day we await a bus to take us to the airport. A Brazilian couple is getting married. They have rented those old-fashioned cars to take their extended family up to a secluded beach for the ceremony. I wish I was a member of this group, beautifully fashioned and turned out for the evening. I would rather be aligned with them than the hundred sad-looking Canadians returning home. I crane my neck to see the bride as she steps from a hot pink car parked in front of the lobby to receive a crying child. The boy wraps his arms around his mother; wipes his snot and tears into her veil, he pulls at her hair. The groom tries to wrench the child, his son maybe, from the bride, but this causes the boy to kick. Finally, she pulls both men into the hot pink car and they drive away on this her special day. I look at B who is also watching the scene and tell him that I want a daughter.

And just like that, it's true.

FLUSH THREE TIMES
TO SHOW YOU CARE

We're like two youngsters. Forever arguing.

I don't remember arguing much with Gert. But Margie. Margie makes me like a pissy child. She's after tapping into some long dormant part of my brain that recalls every injustice I'm after ever suffering. Every favour paid to my brothers that wasn't paid me. Every slight, every sabotage. The opportunities I never had 'cause I didn't go to trade school, the hockey never played 'cause I broke me leg that time, the money I never made 'cause Gert got pregnant in Grade Nine. The fact that Charlie became a mechanic and opened his own garage. Or that Jeremy got hit by a hydro truck and received all that insurance. Jealous: over my own brothers. Stingy: with my own kids. Margie gets all that energy direct. Sometimes we're bawling, arguing with each others' parents like. Sometimes, we are the parents. She becomes Hazel, I become father and these two unrelated people have's a battle in the cab of the truck 'cause of the snow or the speed or the route. Most of the time it's 'cause of the route. I almost put her out on the road when we got lost in Montreal last fall. If we hadn't happened upon the right turnoff accidental like, I knows

I would have, too. She was using that surley tone of her mother's I can't stand. I never heard my own Ma contradict Father once like that. God rest her. But Hazel and Father never fancied one another a day in their lives. Father can't even stand to see the woman in church. They never will get on cause they got nothing in common like. So, I wonders if Margie and I got anything in common. And then I knocks off thinking about that and turns into the back of the couch. Has a nap. I knows I wouldn't love to have a nicer couch.

Sometimes in the evening, or late at night, when we're tired, we mistreats each other. It's like we're right discouraged by our lives and blames it on each other, even though we was hardly handy to one another till two or three year ago. Three year ago. It was three year Christmas past. Resentment is ugly b'y and we're at each other hideous. Two of us—the oldest in our families, too. First born children has some high self-esteem. Feels like a robbery when we don't get our own way. I feels like someone stole me life away from me. Where are my trophies? And all my money? I was supposed to be well respected. I was supposed to have the prettiest wife. The biggest house. A boat! Instead, I got neither one of it. Nothing. And I tells Margie, I should have never brought her out west. I says, I should have left you home with your Jesus mother. Then she tells me she loves me over and over again. Loves me, she do. The sentence slides out of her mouth before she even thinks about saying it. So I tells her she don't, that if she did, she wouldn't be keeping on all the damn time about sending her daughter money for that old medical school. I can't send her daughter money and not send money to my own daughters. Tried that once before. All hell broke loose when the girls found out. Crying. Saying they missed their mother. That I don't love them any more now I got a new woman. And I can't afford to send money to the lot of them. No, no, she says, she really loves me. Loves me so much it makes her crazy. Lord reeving. What am I into?

Margie's drunk on her own proclamations is what's wrong.

Definitely drunk on something. Loaded right full of feelings.
And jealous. Envious every time I smiles at another woman.
Greedy for me. I tells her, she can't be like that. I tries to make
her understand that this is not a quality I admires in her. That
she's a grown woman, not a silly girl. I can no more help smiling
than I can help the colour of my eyes. That's how I was reared
up. To be polite like. But I don't say the right words to make her
understand that, so I has to take her out to *The Keg* for steaks. I
takes her to the stadium one cause she says it got good ambiance.
Margie loves the Winter Grill menu. She'll order everything off
it one go if you mind to let her away with it. Sometimes I do.
I'm right prone to grand gestures like that. Margie's little sister,
Sarah, says it's 'cause of our poverty-stricken heritage. That our
decisions aren't made free. I tells her nothing is free. 'Cept words.
But Sarah already knows that, the way she throws them out in
a room. The three of them loves talking and Sarah talks a mile
a minute. Scared to death her older sisters is going to butt in and
she won't get her say. The drama at their house growing up must
have been enough to drive their father mute. Sure, Free Wareham hardly speaks either word. Not that Hazel will let anyone
else talk, anyway. I prefers quiet, I do. Father was an only child.
He liked a quiet house. My Margie's mind must be some loud
place. I worries I should have never took up with her. She's a
real nice woman, though.

One day she sees a stray dog, right? We're just outside of Edmonton, out in farmland, no houses handy to us. Margie's right
overcome that this dog is gonna freeze. She says, I have more
feelings than any one person should have. So I gives her knee a
little rub like, 'cause it's true. She does. Got her heart wounded
when she was a young one. Now, she's right soft-hearted. Later,
I hears her try the same sentence out on her daughter when she's
on the phone. And then another time, talking to her mother.
So I asks her why do she keep repeating herself? And she says
she was hoping someone would disagree with her. Suggest that
she has just the right amount of feelings. Or that feelings is a
fine thing to have a lot of. Like money. Or integrity. Don't

happen though. Everyone just agrees with her. Then she gets telling me that her Tiffany is nothing like that, right logical-minded. And I'm stunned enough to say she must turn after her father. Sure, everyone knows Lo is the girl's father. But Jesus, don't Margaret go right off the head at me. Tears right into me. And I says give up pretending immaculate conception Margie, we both knows you're no virgin. Now she's not talking to me.

She says I don't show her any love. But I do. I thinks sweeping the floor is a gesture. I thinks washing up the supper dishes shows I care. I always flushes the toilet three times. And I knows that's more than Father ever did. She says that's gross. Not like in her books. That my love is vulgar. Not refined. Not civilized. I'm rural in my heart. She plans me the birthday party she'd like. I does the same. We always ends up with the wrong birthday party. And we aren't young.

But we're not old. We're...adults. Just that. I lost my hair ages ago. She got a tooth gone. Neither one of us is what you would call fit as a fiddle. So what? We're a little broken down. Who cares? We're hurtling forward. I can feel it? The hurtle. 'Cause Margie is impatiently waiting for me to ask her. With jewelry. Barely waiting at all really. Whining to every woman she knows is hardly waiting patiently. The stress of it is making me right shitty. She says, you, you're shitty all the time now. I tries to explain, I already lost my wife. But Margie's nothing like Gert. She's been disappointed so much already. I don't want to disappoint her. But I don't know the first Jesus thing about rings. I don't even know her Jesus finger size.

I suppose, I'll have to phone Hazel. I know she won't make me feel like an old tom cat.

THIS EMPTY HOUSE
IS FULL OF FURNITURE

I never get mail, not good mail, anyway. I mean, I get a scattered take-out menu, electronics store flyer. Visa bill. But nothing good, nothing remarkable. And to think, I almost got excited when I saw that envelope, the high-quality paper. That was until I turned it over. Until I saw the tiny, rigid letters spelling out eight years of my life: first name, middle, last. And I can see him bent over that modern desk, holding an expensive pen, labouring the letters one slow stroke at a time. Everything he does exudes a certain amount of potency, writing a name summons a particular energy, there is an overcast of seething sexuality even in his alphabet. I suppose he wants to ruin my day. Not a chance, shithead, I announce to the mailboxes as I tuck the envelope in my purse, shoving it down amongst a mess of tampons. I wonder how he deals with blood these days.

Inside my apartment, I throw down my purse and decide to ignore it. What do I care? I left him. I'm on my own now, in my own apartment, a one-and-a-half. Fitting, considering my situation. Mao and I are one-and-a-half. There's nothing lonely about living alone if you have a cat...or a television, or in my case, both. I peel back the skin on a chicken thigh while the television mutters from the bedroom and feel grateful they let Martha Stewart out of prison. What odds at all if the woman stole some money? Everybody steals.

I love turnip, it's so wholesome. Mao wraps rings around my legs as he whines for wet food while I wash my one plate and one glass. I can see him standing over a chicken in our old kitchen, rubbing garlic butter along the inside of the bird's thighs, sighing and turning it in his greasy hands. *Slick* is the word that comes to mind when I remember him this way. Full of confidence about cooking. He is slowly searing on the inside. He wishes I would stop talking, but I can't. Our relationship has been smoking for a while, and I've decided to ignore the slow burn. I slip my arms around his waist as he pulls small, red potatoes from the bag.

Want to join some friends in Calgary for the Stampede? A little cattle and binge drinking, hey?

Why would anyone go to Alberta?

He's punching holes into potatoes for a faster cooking time, blindly stabbing away at their small bodies until he mistakes the thin inside of his hand for starch. He has driven a fork through the web of skin between his thumb and forefinger.

Oh my God. Are you okay?

Jesus Christ, Ruth. No! Just get the fuck out of my way!

Our old apartment was so much bigger than where I live now, but you can hardly compare Montreal and St. John's. I said to him, I said, I am moving away, I am going to another province to get away from you, this will never end if I don't. And he said, would that be so bad? Would that be so bad? And he said I was his baby. And he said he'd love me forever no matter where I went. There was nothing I could do to change it, that is what he said. Nothing.

Everything in this apartment is mine. The bonus of living alone is never compromising or asking permission. Can I hang this here? What's wrong with my lamp? I thought you liked yellow. Even still, I worry a little about what he would think of my choices. Would he sigh and shake his head in disgust? A part of me doesn't want him to know what my new home looks like, another part does. The same part that wishes he could imagine me the way I imagine him. Walking around our old living room in the evening holding a mug of ice cream close to his chin, knowing which magazines lie on the floor next to the toilet, smelling sandalwood wafting through the hallway toward the bedroom, our old bedroom. Who sleeps there now? Who goes to Sunday dinner now? Foams the milk for tea and reads the weekend paper a day late. Who does that now? Someone that is not me.

Mao's litter smells funny in the bathroom. There must be something wrong with that cat. I decide to change it and entertain thoughts of opening the envelope. Exchange one pile of shit for another. Cat shit symbolizing independence. We were going to get a cat together, he said. I don't need you to get a cat. I'll get my own damn cat. Absurd. As if a cat meant I was over it. Meanwhile, I still compare all men to him. He is my fixed reference point by which to judge all men—new, old, otherwise. Even now, knowing that we can never be together after that envelope is opened, I am also aware that I will continue to think of him this way 'cause I am a loser. Knowing fully that this cannot be a healthy tendency, but still knowing that eight years cannot be erased from my mind. There is something to be said for complete and ultimate amnesia: I'll wish for it on a shooting star, when I blow out my candles, at every opportunity.

The phone is ringing. It's Emily. She probably received an envelope too, probably wants to dish about the contents over a can of beer. I don't, as this would involve admitting that I haven't opened it. Aha! Emily, with this tidbit of information, will turn her psychoanalyst bullshit on blast, and I cannot suffer through another one of those conversations; a mere repeat of the same one we've been having since I moved here.

But that can only mean you still love him. Just admit this is a possibility.

I will admit no such thing—not to Emily, not to myself, not to God. I'd rather watch YouTube with Mao, in my dirty gym clothes, until it's dark. Hell, I won't even get up to turn on a light. Instead, I'll negotiate my way around the apartment by computer screen. Utterly depressing. There is an email from my sister in Truro: when will I come visit, spend some time with my niece? When I have airline fare, I write back. That should shut her up for a while. Keep her silent in case I'm hinting she loan me money. Family is so predictable. His family will be overjoyed by the news, no doubt ecstatic that I'm finally out of the picture. As if I was somehow the mastermind behind his poor performance as a man. Yes, certainly I'm to blame for his temper, his disrespect of others, his outright ignorance. Somehow I had instilled these qualities in him before we ever met and was just minding my time for eight years, preparing to expose him for the foul-mouthed, obnoxious fuck-up he really was. All things—everywhere—my fault.

But Emily is relentless. She has left messages on my Facebook wall so that everyone can see me hiding. And I wonder what are they saying back home. Facebook is crack for the wounded. I know, I know I should delete him but I can't. It's too...finite. Instead, I'll look at pictures of him smiling with friends, lit up like a firecracker, on an old couch in a room above the Grapevine. This is the guy who broke my heart, the guy who chose that over me. I can handle these pictures, they're confirmation of making the right decision. The adult decision.

It's the new pictures that make me ache, make me angry, flood me with the piss and vinegar of a woman scorned. At home with her, eating dinner with her, folding laundry with her.

Outside during the day with her, snowshoeing, snowmobiling! Sometimes I fill up with a revolutionary hatred for having wasted all my pretty years waiting for him to grow up, having invested so much emotional currency in a guy who had no intentions of being any kind of man. The bank of Ruth is empty, I spent it all on him, and now I'm thirty. He stole my twenties and now the thought of dating someone new, with a whole new set of problems, overwhelms me. Even considering being naked in front of another man makes me want to puke. Goddamn it, I hate them all. What am I going to do now? I'll clean the bathroom, again. May as well be close to the can in case I actually vomit this time. Spinning the toilet brush around the toilet rim, thinking of a time when he would sit on the seat while I took a bath, watch me shave my legs, content to have me listen to him pore over his day. The relationship was over when I started shutting the door. The thought of him seeing me naked through the clear curtain brought on an unexplainable feeling of uncleanliness. He sensed it and he stopped visiting. There were no more conversations about glazed ham over Ivory bubbles. And I miss him...a little...for a second. Even if I'm not allowed to. Or don't want to.

Mao wakes me around five because he's starving, or at least he thinks he's starving. Not that the morbidly obese Chairman could starve in a week, possibly even two. He's a dynasty of house cats, unrelenting in his overindulgence, and I can no more say no to him than I can stop chewing my nails. Bitten to the cusps of being painful, I can feel him staring at me across the island, across the Straits, through the bottom of Labrador. I can feel the judgment every time I gnaw.

That's gross, Ruth. You're so fucking gross.

I remember the constant disappointment tailing my every decision, keeping me in line. I have to remember, remind myself of these things, so I don't think of those other things. Sweet things. I try to do everything in spite of him. I painted my apartment grey because he hates the fog, named the cat Mao because he has a strong dislike for China. Everything is slightly informed by him and it rots me. Like that damn envelope peeking out of my purse, watching me slurp the remaining milk from my cereal bowl. Probably thinking I'm immature. Probably daring me to open it. Nope! No sir, not today. Not on my day off. Saturday. Maybe Monday. Monday sucks anyway. I'm gonna paint today, get some work done, be productive. I will. But I don't. Instead, I reorganize my scrapbooks, far more productive use of my time. I slide all photos of us together behind other photos. My scrapbooks will be a reflection of a time before him when I was more myself than at present. They will be a travel guide to where I am headed, my own little lonely planet. But Emily Blanchard cannot be ignored, buzzing the intercom for recognition. Gawd. I press the speak button.

I know you're in there. I can smell you through the intercom. You reek of self-pity.

I don't know why I let her in. She flops down on my red futon with as much drama as the colour can muster. She looks wired in her deep orange sundress, buttons marching up her middle, opened just enough to introduce her breasts to the city. A frown crosses her lips when she eyes the scrapbooks all over the floor, and I can already hear her commenting. Emily is surveying the wreck, filing away my love life as she might any other case study. Social workers are so exhausting, social work students even more so. It is only ten and Emily has obviously already maxed out her caffeine credit for the day. Starbucks should have her banned for public safety.

And what exactly is this supposed to accomplish, anyway?
I haven't thought that far ahead yet.
Well, I suggest you do 'cause as far as I can tell, you're obsessing.
Obsession has such negative connotations.
So does denial, Ruth.

Why am I friends with such a heartless bitch? A human being with so little tact. It was Emily who, just months ago, demanded that we go for coffee, had an announcement that could not wait until after class. Somewhere in the depths of her soul, Emily thought it appropriate to tell me in the middle of the street. We were headed toward Second Cup on St. Denis, people watching, window-shopping. I had been unprepared, ambushed. This, I thought, is how the French must have felt.

He's living with someone.
Living with someone?
There's something else.
Who is he living with?
I don't know her but listen...
Who is she? What's she like?
No one's met her but...she's young.
How young?
Like, in her early twenties or something.
Early twenties?

I had been in my twenties once, in my early twenties when we met. He is sick, he is twisted. He is certainly not over us yet, is he? How could he be? We had spent so much time together, so much time breaking up, months of saying goodbye daily, only for him to run out and replace me with some young one. It's disrespectful. He has abandoned the grave of our relationship leaving me alone to grieve. Hadn't he emailed that he still loved me just a week before? Hadn't he called?

Hey, how are you?
Fine. How are you?
Good. I was thinking we need to have a face to face.
Why?
I have some things I need to say to you.
I bet you do.
Please?
I don't think that would be appropriate.

Why not?

Listen, I gotta go. I'm at Ikea.

Ikea? Again? You should have them come by to photograph your apartment for their next catalogue.

Sure, whatever. I'll call you.

Hadn't called him though. Met a boy instead. A tall French boy with a broken arm to match his broken glasses. Met at the Musee d'Art Contemporian during a Brian Jungen exhibit while standing under a whale skeleton made entirely of plastic lawn chairs, both arching our necks under the modern, prehistoric beast. We stumbled into one another and he said...

Jungen's assemblages suggest how, in the global marketplace, cultural identification and aspiration increasingly collapse into forms of brand recognition.

I had read this online too, but I allowed him his moment of thievery. Everybody steals, and besides, what a random thing to say considering English was his second language. Dressed in black runners, jeans, white T-shirt; he was so casual. I had a brief fling with the plagiarist, spent evenings walking around the Plateau, eating baguettes and drinking cheap, red, tetra-pack wine. It was a pinch cliché, but it was a distraction. Making nervous eyes at a handsome French sculptor in Quebec until his arm healed and he returned to work. It was nothing really. We never even...I was never his girlfriend. A diversion maybe, but nothing more. A mere fiction. Emily said his not calling back was for the best. Dr. Blanchard feels transference is unhealthy. Starting tomorrow, I promise myself to actively seek out new friends.

Emily grabs the purse up and digs out the envelope, waves it suggestively around, places it to her forehead and squeezes her eyes tight. She knows the contents. She is performing for me, searching for a bit of humour in the horror of it. Emily doesn't believe in dwelling. She believes in drinking.

Fine. Fine then. I need a drink. Let's get hammer-loaded tonight.

Right.

But you have to open it tomorrow. Hang it all over in one day. Sunday.

Sure.

So the envelope is placed on the coffee table. A suggestive reminder of reality amongst the free arts rags. I am certain I can do better than most of the crap inside. I am certain but held in place by the fear that maybe...I can't. Never really trying keeps my delusion of untapped potential alive, as if never trying and never failing were married to one another. Besides, I don't really have time to concentrate on painting right now. I'm in the middle of studying the work of others rather than making my own. I had a small enough amount of success to warrant moving to the mainland to pursue grander opportunities. Home is unaware of my stagnancy, moving in itself being a worthwhile accomplishment. Walking along Mont Royal thinking, I can never live in Newfoundland again. I have forsaken my brethren, I have been forsaken. All these thoughts are a tad dramatic, I know, but they're still valid. How can I live there now?

I always say goodbye to a place as if I'll never see it again. My impending death weighing heavy on my shoulders each time I board a flight. I know that you can never return to a place, that over time it will morph into a new town with a new scene. New regulars. But there are days when I let myself wallow in the grief of understanding that I will never walk into summer 2003 again. Fresh from my first degree, infatuated with him, holding my future in front of me like a surprise egg. The chocolate hiding something small and wonderful; possibility safely inside for my consumption. Emily doesn't think on these things. She has a suspicious distaste for nostalgia. Emily is a creature of the now—always outfitted in the hottest new fashion trend. Tube scarves, audio books, ordering the hippest cocktail of the day. Not me. I will not be swayed by the hype, steadfast in my dedication to black A-lines and dark lager. Probably why I was with him so long in the first place. I had decided on him. He was my man whether he liked it or not. Maybe it's all my fault, after all.

Emily always saying, your parents are so obviously still together.
Me thinking, your parents are so obviously not.

How can Emily make that statement as if it has negative ramifications? She has a superiority complex directly related to her parents' divorce. Children from broken homes think themselves stronger; Emily feels her independence is a direct result of what she *went through.* Her parents' troubled marriage being some sort of test of character that she has passed with remarkable ease. She plans on passing on her acquired wisdom within the social justice sphere. Emily will have everyone legally separated for the children. She is musing about the homeless situation over sangria, ice quickly disappearing in the pitcher. I wish could melt away.

Have you eaten anything today?

Food is a chore on days like this. I'd prefer a pill, an injection of protein, a shot of your daily required vitamins and minerals. And I'm shiny under my grey tank top, a slow river of sweat explores the space between my tits, snaking its way along my back to the very tip of my tailbone, the crack of my ass. He would say, I love the sweet smell of your sweat. Your candy-apple armpits. He would say, you are what they mean when they say sugar and spice. Asshole.

Ruth, where are you? Who are you with?

Emily is frowning again, pulling back her dirty blonde curls, up and away from her neck. Emily is beautiful, is something deserving of unabashed stares. Emily, a paper-bag princess, the kind of girl that can make even oilskins look sexy. I am not that kind of girl—or, at least, not today. Emily wants to talk about it.

Let's go to the park, let's brown bag it. Come on.

In the park, lush and innocent, the smell of another summer's worth of grass just waking up. Rested. I wish I could grow myself a new skin, mow myself down so that his fingerprints wouldn't be all over me. Forensics would be stumped when I turned up dead. This young woman has never been touched! Emily asking over beers at Thanksgiving, can I tell Ruth? His response: I don't care. It's none of her business. None of my business? What happened to *I'll love you forever?* What happened to *you'll always be my baby?* And I can feel him cutting himself out of my life forever. He has sealed this in an envelope with his own spit. One last gesture at hate. A last stab at heartbreak. Marriage would have less permanence but that is not his style. He is a student of the clean-slate school of relationships. He will reinvent himself—new girl, new career, new friends. I won't get to know him or even hear second-hand information about him. All because I left. My choice.

Ruth?
He erased me.
Jesus, Ruth. He hasn't erased you. He...replaced you.
Am I a fucking coffee pot, a vacuum cleaner, a spaniel puppy? Do you just replace people?
Some people do.

The hippies are becoming aware of the setting sun. They're off to their reggae parties; they will beat the drums in someone's backyard tonight. Emily says she honestly has no time for hippies. The wine is bringing out the less diplomatic parts of her personality. She thinks it's a question of hygiene. I'm relieved she has abandoned her quest to search the empty cabinets of my heart. I doubt you'd even find a saltine at this point. Emily is scanning through her text messages, looking for a party. She is sure she is invited to at least one this evening. Turns out, there's actually three.

Choice, she says, lends itself to getting hammer-loaded. We will trek around to all three parties but first we must obtain a Manon.

Manon being Emily's French-Canadian, poet friend with a penchant for hauling lines and swiping sunglasses.

I do not pay for sunglasses, they are meant to be free for my face.

Manon will keep us on course tonight. She will not allow us to veer off into Newfoundland; she will ground us in Quebec and all things French. She meets us at the corner of Hotel de Ville and Marianne. She has been drinking on a musician's balcony all afternoon; a svelte, handsome hipster who may just be the next big thing. She tries not to sound impressed by his recent success. She tosses off that he has been trying to sleep with her for years. She just throws this information away as if she were butting out a cigarette. I will acquire this easy cool nature of Manon's. I will succeed in being French and fucking rock stars.

Manon says the upside to being a starving artist is thinness. In a bathroom, hours later, we're laughing at girls from Toronto. We're our bitchiest selves under the circumstances. He wouldn't think this was funny. He'd say, for every person you are talking about, there are ten people talking about you. I share this last bit with the girls.

Manon squeals, yelling, we will be very popular? Infamous, yeah? Her volume control has been compromised by the ketamine and she doesn't give a shit. We consider returning to the party, but decide to hole up in the bathroom until someone finds us. A deer crossing the road would be far more efficient than time moving forward. Manon has accidentally flushed responsibility down the toilet. Emily mentions the letter, its flushability.

Here, my little Anglo friend. Take this and screw a stranger. It will help things.

I find fault in Manon's logic and decide to head home. The sun is already pulling itself out of bed. This type of behaviour is ridiculous, I think, as my body temperature hops and dips, curves and spins red rings over my cheekbones. I feel my brain melting and remember the envelope. Mao is sitting on the coffee table next to it. Does everyone think I should open it? Fine, they will all be responsible. Emily, Manon, even Mao. But especially him. Sending it was a stroke of evil fucking genius.

Invited. To the baptism. Our first child.
Shawn Joseph Edgar Macaulay, Jr..

And I see him reading *The New Yorker* on the back deck, drinking a glass of white wine and grilling salmon, shaving in the bathroom mirror, all the doors and windows, open. There's Nivea For Men aftershave, there's Big Macs and cartoons on the sofa. Dinner parties and group vacations; gift exchanges, him driving us home from the mall. And there's the last time I saw him.

He said he saw you making out with some fat chick at a party!
Ruth, we were totally messed up.
You're always totally messed up.
What's your fucking problem Ruth?
You are! You're my fucking problem. But not for long. We're over. Spend all night, every night, at your skinny friend's shit apartment for all I care. Sleep there. Someone should get some sleep somewhere. I mean, I probably won't sleep tonight cause I am so fucking angry at you, again. Because I've been had, again. Continually believing a fiendish drunk who sleeps until work and drinks until dawn. Jesus, fucking, fuck Shawn! I won't miss being out with my boyfriend in the daytime because we never are. Ever. And, and I'm gonna put warm sheets on my bed for the winter and eventually, when I've stopped being so pissed at myself for wasting my twenties on you, I'll sleep alone in them

comfortably. Don't call or try to see me. I hate you. You broke my heart.

And he's throwing an iced cappuccino at me across Duckworth Street. And he's saying, I never want to see you again in my life you crazy bitch.

Of all the names in the world, he's giving this girl's baby his. And now I'm crying. I want to break him into little pieces. I want to snap the bones in his fingers and toes. I want to hurt him all at once the same amount he hurt me over eight years. I want to tear up this information, to make it untrue, to never know it. I want to think that there still might be a chance for happiness with him, but how can there be now that he has run off and started a family, our family, with some other girl? After everything he put me through, he owes me. Would that be so bad? Would it? Yes, it would have. It would have. I know that and yet I am still crawling on my knees, weeping to the point of near asphyxiation, snot running down my face onto the floor, scaring the cat. I am desperate, I need to speak to him, I need to tell him what he has done over and over and over and over until I don't need to tell him ever again. He owes me an audience. He will listen. I will make him listen to my heartache long distance.

Hello.
I opened it.
Oh, Ruth.
I'm all alone.
You're not alone. You have me. I'm coming over. Don't move, don't do anything. I'll bring bagels.
Okay, hurry.

And I love Emily. She's my best friend.

THESE CANADIAN CHILDREN ARE NOT MINE

Alexi lets out a thick moan before heaving himself aside. He kisses the palm of his right hand and pats Tanya's face. She waits, barely breathing, clenching her pillow until she is certain of his deep sleep and then sobs into the sleeve of her flannel nightgown. I hate Canada, she thinks. The family had migrated over two years ago. Alexi had promised to leave his vices in the motherland; he had bribed her with democracy, opportunity and freedom, but Tanya cannot find these things here. She just finds more of the same. Cheap women still stand on the corner of their street and the bridge that carries Alexi to his job crumbles a little every day. She fears that he will die trying to make his way to the sex toy warehouse where he drives a forklift for minimum wage. The thought of this is as humiliating as it is terrifying for Tanya. At least in Russia he had worked for a respectable business. She refuses to remember the kind of products he hoists whenever asked; she claims she can't recall. Something very French, she says. Alexi feels no such embarrassment; rather, he regales all who will listen with tales of buttplugs spilling from damaged containers. This kind of thing he discusses with great enthusiasm at the dinner table, in front of their children.

Regardless, Montreal is still far better than where they were first settled. Thinking of St. John's brings bile to Tanya's throat. She can taste her loathing for the barren little town with its fat women and lack of delis. Because it was a little town by Russian standards, even if it did refuse to acknowledge this fact. Tanya despised how the infertile-feeling rock was ruefully unapologetic about itself. At least at home, Tanya thought, people were smart enough to be disappointed. She had worked temporarily at a fried chicken establishment that specialized in selling awful food to the hungover. She had tried it only twice. The first time she had brought it home to celebrate her new job, though it had made her family sluggish and irritable. The children had argued over the television and Alexi had snarled at Tanya when she mentioned the landlord's phone call. And to think she had paid money for this food. She vowed never to eat it again. The second time she ate it she was trying to fit in with her co-work-ers. They had been offended when she hadn't eaten lunch with them, so as an act of solidarity she ate a chicken sandwich, after which she spent most of her shift running to the bathroom with terrible bowels. This too had been an issue for the heavy women of Newfoundland, Tanya's insistence on moving her bowels when the urge struck her. Apparently, in that foggy heathen place, you were expected to hold feces in your person for long periods of time rather than use any toilet outside of your pri-mary residence. Tanya thinks this likely contributes to their miserable lot in life. Holding all that shit in. She was so re-lieved when the family finally moved to Montreal. There had been flowers and Alexi had said, see, this is real Canada.

But here her son Valery complains of having a girl's name and Rozalina refuses to eat Tanya's cooking. She wants cheese curds and gravy on her potatoes if she *must* eat more starch. Tanya is horrified when boys call looking for *Val*. She tells them no one by that name lives at this number, until her son gets angry, so she stops answering the telephone altogether. It only brought about frustration anyway, she thinks, trying to make sense of the thick Québécois accents. Alexi buys Tanya

French lessons for her birthday. He wants her to meet French women, make friends, enjoy—or so he says. But Tanya feels sure that he has suddenly grown bored with her old ways; disgusted by the sponginess of her middle, ashamed of her fur collars. It's not right to wear fur in Canada, Rozalina says. Your jewellery is too much, Valery insists. Please practice speaking *en français*, Alexi goes on and on and on. It all makes Tanya weary.

Valery and Rozalina start speaking French in front of their mother. When Tanya mentions this to Alexi, he mumbles something about incentive. But Tanya is certain the children do not say kind things. They speak in the loose, broken language of their peers while they watch Tanya knead lumps out of bread. She asks them to speak Russian around Mommy; she says she is lonely for home but Rozalina says she is selfish, not wanting them to improve. You do not want us to make friends, Rozalina says, heading toward the room she shares with her brother. These are not my children, Tanya thinks, these Canadian children are not mine. She imagines her sweet Russian babes chewing pumpkin Oladi, rubbing vanilla along their aching gums, the price no matter. In Russia, Alexi would have raged at hearing Roza speak to her mother this way. But here it is okay, it is normal to disrespect your mother in Canada.

Her family watches hockey in the living room. Apparently, they are now Habs fans. Roza has brought a friend over to watch with them. This young, black man has arrived empty-handed and had to be told to remove his shoes before tracking all of Montreal North in on his soles. He compliments Tanya on her framed photograph of Saint Basil's, which she in turn offers to him as a gift. The young man accepts immediately and Tanya is horrified. The Habs lose and Gillies leaves with her cathedral tucked under his arm. Tanya is appalled and takes her despair out on her daughter, who explains at great length to stop offering their possessions to guests. Tanya calls Gilles a thief and is accused of being a racist. Tanya? A racist?

Tanya walks to the clinic in her neighbourhood. Alexi pestered her to ask after some pills for her sadness. A nurse informs her that the medication would be quite expensive without a Québec health card. She gives Tanya forms in French; the whole ordeal takes hours and ends in tears. Alexi thinks she should go to emergency for the pills but Tanya is too tired. She does not tell him this. Instead, she smiles and says she is feeling much better, just needing air. Alexi is reassured, kisses his palm and pats her face. He will walk Roza to a friend's for dinner, would she like to come? *Neet, neet.* She kisses her palm and pats Alexi's cheek as he pulls on his coat. His new Canadian coat. Grey and very boring Tanya thinks, and she wonders why everyone is so quick to forget Russia. Russia is a kind of death, Alexi proclaims. Why is Russian not good enough anymore, Tanya wonders, as cold air rushes into their apartment.

But Russian is good enough for some things, Tanya thinks, as Alexi crawls into bed, hands groping for the tail of her nightgown. She shows little interest, she allows it to happen. Alexi mutters, sucks, pinches and prods in many languages and Tanya feels like a whore bedding multiple men. She pulls her nightgown around her knees when Alexi has finished and curls into the same position her children had favoured as babes. Instead of sucking her thumb, she reaches inside the neck of her nightgown and envelops her breast in her palm. She hates it here but she does not think she will be here long. She has told Alexi to send for her younger sister because she is lonely. Tanya has seen the way Alexi looks at her eager sister. It will be better this way, Tanya thinks, as she comforts herself, kneading the hard little lump between her fore and middle finger, telling no one of it because she doesn't have the words.

SOME WORDS TASTE BETTER THAN OTHERS

Leon

She didn't read the menu. Instead, she stared at it deliber-ately. Admiring the font and mouthing the words at me. Long-ingly. *Maple glaze. Cream sauce.* She rolled them over her tongue, tasting each before expelling them onto the table like you would bad pieces of fish. Her face read disdain. And she ordered a salad. She says sometimes she adds an egg or chicken for protein. Never red meat, never dairy, never dessert. An obvious left-over eating disorder. I encouraged her to try mine.

The night she walked into the bar, I wanted to know her right away. I didn't ask her name but I should have.

She walked in with a group of shellacked thirty-somethings. A bachelorette. Or a birthday, maybe. There was a pink feather boa, there was a dollar store tiara. She ordered a vodka soda with lime and asked if England wasn't depressing enough for me. Why here, she wondered aloud as she licked lime juice from her thumb and forefinger. I told her I followed a girl to Toronto. She

75

nodded knowingly and said she'd followed a guy to Korea once. I told her I had my heart broken the first time in Asia. She said *me too* and walked away. Later, I watched her dance in her naked feet. I promised myself I'd get her number. But the whole affair ended with the bride or birthday girl crying in a bathroom stall while her friends coaxed her out with promises of party favours that would *straighten her right up*. The nameless girl, a woman really, still in her naked feet called some Deborah a whore. And then they were all gone, with incredible urgency, to drink and dance privately in some Ellen's living room.

Finally I saw her again outside of a gym downtown. Weeks later. She had a gym bag thrown over her shoulder, curly hair plastered against her face. Sweat everywhere. And she was smoking. Her friend, the bride or birthday girl, was working herself into a frenzy, waving her hands, punctuating sentences with gusts of smoke. *The cops,* the friend yelled and people turned toward the conversation. We all stared. The pair of them turned to face the wall, laughing. The friend said, *give me another cigarette for god's sake, Ellen.* And I knew. Just like that. Her name was Ellen. It was her living room they had danced in.

I asked about her and was told she was a hard ticket. Has four brothers. Is from the bay. Stay clear of her, my manager said. But she's got a thing for me. So I didn't follow her advice. Crazy, said another co-worker. But he thinks all women everywhere are crazy. So I didn't follow his advice, either. My roommate said to stop asking people for advice I had no intention of following. It's annoying, he said. He suggested to just find out where she works and drop by under some pretence. She works at an ad agency. I tried to manufacture a pretense.

I came up with no pretense.

Then I was drunk on a Monday. Martini Monday. Homesick. Sulking. Somewhat hating women until her friend walked in. She looked very tired and very wide awake. She was loaded.

I exaggerated my own drunkenness though I had a strong foundation to work from. I explained. I told her. Asia broke our hearts. Chrome-coloured toenails. Something about fate. And then my roommate interrupted before I said too much. He got the number and I memorized it in the cab on the way home. He let me call her twice. The second time, I asked her to dinner. She suggested meeting for drinks. On Saturday. Later my roommate locked himself in the bathroom with our cellphones and the landline. He explained, while taking a shit, that I'd freak her out if I called too often. Newfoundland girls, he said, spook easily.

Every day I wait for Saturday.

Ellen

He tells me some random story about why he no longer listens to Bob Marley. It's the second time he has called me in so many days. I respond by explaining why all reggae is stupid. I don't mean this to sound crass, but it does. This means I'm nervous. There is no reason to be nervous. I can't even remember meeting him at Kim's birthday. But he remembers me, which makes me more nervous. This always takes me by surprise. The fact that someone, a man, wants to take me to dinner. I don't like eating in public so I suggest drinks. My neighbourhood familiar. Dark and sour with its forever broken toilets and bartenders I know. It'll be okay. Everything will be fine.

Everything is not fine. I'm late because I don't have any clothes. I mean, I have clothes. But everything I own is too big or too small. Too much or not enough. Why don't I own fucking basics? I settle on a black shirt that plunges in the back. Backs are sexy, right? Dark blue jeans. Brown oxfords. A leather jacket that my mother thinks looks severe. I think severe sounds like a safe look for a half-blind date. He is sitting in the window with a girl I know from George Street. I know it is him because he said he would wear a hat and he is the only man in the bar wearing a hat. A plaid newsboy cap which I think looks ridiculous and worry is hiding a misshapen, bald head. I drink five glasses of red wine on an empty stomach and rejoice when I discover he has hair. I drink two more glasses and tell him my top ten worst stories. I show him my abscessed tooth. I tell him I owe student loans $32,000. I tell him I once gave my whole family crabs. I tell him that's a lie. After another glass of wine, I tell him it's true again.

I have no time for shame, guilt or regret, I say. I resist the urge. Also, self-pity and dependence. Both a waste of time. I demand to know where his Toronto girlfriend is. There was a girlfriend in Toronto, wasn't there? Or a wife? I tell him bluntly that I have no interest in other people's boyfriends. I tell him I'm not one of those girls. He laughs a lot. He keeps up to me. He confesses his ambition. He gestures to my hair. He leans in often and I excuse myself to the bathroom before he ever makes contact. I am a hot mess. A poor first date. And I leave without saying goodbye.

Shockingly, he asks me to dinner and I accept.

I'm not nervous anymore. There's nothing left to do but be myself. He orders too much food. I don't order enough. We share. It's altogether pleasant. And suddenly, I want it to be nice. I want it to work out. I allow that little tingle in my abdomen to expand. I remind myself that I'm not dead, just thirty-four. People can still fall in love at thirty-four. And I will myself to not fuck it up. I wish I had shaved my legs. Next time. And there will be a next time because this beautiful Englishman sitting across from me, who has perfect teeth and his own house, looks at me like he wants to eat me.

And I feel delicious.

FRENCH KISSING IS
FOR TEENAGERS

Fuck your fence lady.

Janine barks at the thirty-something yuppie who called the police on her. She wasn't hurting the precious fence, just using it to prop up a tarp sheltering her from the daily summer showers. She buttoned up after the one remark, though; didn't need to be thrown in lock-up again. Janine promised herself she would learn more French before that ever happened. Tabarnac, indeed. What was she going to do now? Surely, she will die of pneumonia if she continues to get soaked every day. Montreal would be a breeze, they said, beautiful city, beautiful weather, great spot to start out anew.

They had been starting out anew; a team working toward something bigger and better than a bungalow in Windsor, Ontario. Janine was still aching over the whole affair, depleted of whatever will she had. Worn out. Him eyeing her because she'd let milk go bad in the fridge, pushing her toward the litter box, always pointing that accusing finger in her face because she was so wrong. Now what is she left with? A violin and a broken heart. The cat even ran away.

I am just going to keep getting angrier until you come home. This is not going to work.

Walking through Parc Lafontaine with tears rolling down her cheeks, sliding out from under her sunglasses, she occasionally reaches up to wipe a couple away. Ten years and she was the girl who did everything wrong. Janine had tried to mend her mistakes; alter her behaviour, thinking that she could force out an ounce of perfection. If he preferred vanilla ice cream then she would buy vanilla ice cream. If he felt she should get up when he did then she would get up when he did. She could do these things: so Canadian, a real peacekeeper. But soon enough he would claim he had never liked vanilla ice cream, didn't she know that? Rolling his eyes in that "you are so stupid" manner he had perfected. Janine would spend countless hours standing amongst the grocery store aisles wondering what he would prefer to eat. What food would make Simon happy?

But food could not make Simon happy. Janine could not make Simon happy, either. Simon was the only person who could make Simon happy and he just wasn't having any of it. *Only simpletons are happy. Only teenagers french kiss. Only. Only. Only.* He would be infuriated by whatever Janine did or said; all thoughts and opinions were as insufficient as no thoughts and opinions. Berating of the highest calibre took place in shopping malls, restaurants, the street and at some point, Janine no longer had any desire to leave the house. Until the day she did. The locked door and pulled curtains were suffocating her. His weary eyes and frustrated voice exhausted her, so she packed a reusable shopping bag: two oranges, a pack of blueberries, four slices of bread. And she left him. She went to a friend's, slept in a single bed, eventually got the cat back, cried, missed him, felt guilty and lonely—especially at night.

It's a matter of deciding what you can and cannot live with. Can you live with being a sad person?

Then Mr. Doyle, her tabby, ran away, and her friend

demanded she get over it. As if there is an expiration date on grief and poverty. Some unspoken time limit on her misery. Her friend hounded her about her dirty hair and suggested she should go on a date. As a distraction. As if Janine knew what a date was, as if she hadn't gleefully chosen to forget that information when Simon asked her to move in with him. It would help her to move on, they all said. Janine decided to embrace this notion physically. Isn't that what he said she had been doing all along? Running from their problems? Well, fine. She'd run. Which is how she ended up leaning on some well-dressed woman's fence for support. She had abandoned her life, no longer recognizing her routine, herself. Stolen glimpses in clothing store windows hinted at the dark bags under her eyes, as she quickly moved along. Janine walked with purpose without destination; she found it comforting. Her skin still betrayed how exhausted she actually was, so she tried to avoid it as best she could. But reflections can be found anywhere in the plateau. Janine thought she might move to the canal area where reflections are rare and mostly forgiving. The water shifting and the concrete ignoring her. The Lachine Canal: a perfect place to disappear.

Janine reaches into her pockets as she walks southwest toward the canal. She becomes distraught when she pulls out a lone twenty. Even her money is desolate. She thought there would be more and wonders where her last hundred dollars has gone. She grieves for it the way a hungry person gnaws at an apple core. There was the new underwear. Splurging on fruit. A bus ticket from Toronto. Why had she taken the bus from Toronto?

Her father was the reason she took the bus from Toronto. Janine is sitting at the kitchen table. She is eating toast covered in butter and raspberry jelly, dipping it in her tepid, milky tea. Her dad is reading the paper when he suddenly looks at her, demanding her focus. Butter and tea run down her chin and drop onto her lap, staining her pink sweatpants. Janine is worried her mother will be mad, having gotten her clothes dirty before even going to school. But her mother is preoccupied with finding her little brother who hates Grade One. *Jinny, promise you will never hitchhike. Girls who hitchhike will most certainly be raped. Promise me.* And her nine-year-old self promised, kept her promise long after her father was dead. All the men on the line smoked in those days.

Janine had bought the bus ticket to Montreal and now she was properly fucked. A nasty yeast infection has been plaguing her for the last three nights; she is certain she will lose her mind if she doesn't get some sleep soon. Even generic medication would clean her out of at least a tenner and there was no guarantee it would work. She considers shoplifting and is reminded of her night in lock-up. She passes a group of trans kids on Saint Laurent. She had tried hanging out with similar groups for safety's sake but they had rejected her. She is too old, too poor, too depressing. She never has drugs or anything to drink. Once she intervened when she thought a girl was being assaulted. The girl and her boyfriend were not impressed. This was when Janine decided to go it alone, decided to leave Ontario. Everyone in Toronto thought she was mentally ill anyway. Or a crackhead. Or a whore. You had to be one of these things if you were over thirty and living on the streets of Toronto. Janine wanted to ask them if you couldn't just be unhappy. Or lost. Really, desperately lost. But she didn't. They wouldn't have listened anyway.

I love you. Things will be different, better, I promise. I put a battery in your watch.

She called him before leaving Ontario to let him know that she was okay. She said that she realized now it was not his fault. She said he wasn't to blame. He cried and begged her to come home. He described the lilacs in the yard, he said her peas were coming up, he murmured he would try so much harder. This. Time. She asked him to bring lilacs to her mother and hung up. Her mother didn't really know what was going on. Simon said Janine was away for training, a work thing. Mary had become increasingly suspicious after a time; she had gone to the police. Janine found this comical. Her mother never was a huge fan of her husband. Why had she gotten married so young? Probably because of her dad's lung cancer, because it seemed like something she could do without a lot of effort, because Simon made her cum. Maybe it was because of the ongoing, everlasting fight with her mother or because she failed her accounting classes —every last one. Likely it was because she was in love...and happy. She wanted her daddy to walk her down the aisle. Ten years ago she had been a very pretty bride. Now she smelled of sweat and her vagina was itchy. An equally unhappy-looking Anglo woman gives her five dollars. Her abrasive friend, in a correspondingly vulgar orange sundress, comments that Janine will likely waste it on meth. Janine snaps that she's saving up for Monostat and the friendly one quickly ducks into a pharmacy for the cure. She says she takes antibiotics a lot. Janine thinks she's probably Irish.

Later Janine meets a group of travelling musicians on Saint Catherine. They are going to Atlantic Canada. She has never been, but she really likes fish. They'll pay for her ferry and food, they say, if she'll play her violin. An extra violin won't go astray, they assure her, as Easterners are apparently wild for a fiddle. She will get to keep the violin and leave Montreal. It all seems like a good idea at the time. But she hates the dark highways of New Brunswick and vomits her way across the Gulf as the retro-upholstered ferry heaves itself from side to side. Janine wonders why these people don't build a bridge or dig a tunnel. Something. Anything would be better than this. This is transportation from the stone ages, Janine thinks, as she wipes her mouth in her sleeve. She will regret this decision horribly as she spends the next week hitching the Trans-Canada 1 smelling sour. Newfoundland's climate matches the temperature of her heart. Rain, drizzle and fog every day. Janine wonders who would ever want to live in such a place.

And they drink, these *islanders*. They drink until their eyes cross and they're spitting on the floor. The men scare her, the women as much or more. She can hardly understand them, what with their mouths full of cigarettes and slurred speech. She had seen lots of drunk people when she worked at the casino, but this was something else entirely. The same people she sees with cocaine hanging out of their nose at night will walk by her on the street the next morning as if she isn't there. One day she overhears a guy wonder aloud *where all these fucking transients came from* as he hauls on a king-size and sips an espresso, while playing chess outside of a coffee shop. Janine has seen him late at night fighting with his girlfriend—or wife, she could even be his wife—underneath an awning while their friends carry on binge drinking. Yelling hysterically at your spouse on Water Street is no big deal to these people. Janine thinks they're all nuts, every one of them. These people who hang clothes out on a cold February morning. And the fish is expensive, too.

She decides to try a shelter, but that is worse still. The women are battered, addicted to Oxycontin and hateful. She sleeps with her violin under her shirt to prevent thievery, or worse, attempts to play it. Newfoundlanders all think they're musically inclined. They're not. Janine cries more than ever and wishes after Montreal, after Toronto, after Windsor and her bungalow. She watches women, just like the kind of woman she was, cycle toward a better self-image and misses shaving her legs. She is cold all the time and hates fucking Ziggy's. And the fucking hills and all these fucking drunk people everywhere she looks. And why aren't there any payphones in this goddamn city! She finally finds one on a corner, dials and stares at a cruise ship while she waits for that absent click. Germans. Or Swedes maybe. She thinks they'll be disappointed if they stay too long. Click.

Baby? It's me. I want to come home.

SINGLE GALS NEED
ALL WHEEL DRIVE

A heartbroken Newfoundland man is completely void of original thought. So thinks Kim.

He exhibits no creativity and sees no correlation between moving on and growing up. These two sentiments are totally unrelated. Moving on being the primary focus. Of course. Distance is the thing he's after. The space between, like that horrible song, is the clichéd reality of Kim's new-found knowledge. She, like many women before and after her, will be secured firmly in the past in a full-throttle drive to get back to *normal*. Normal being any state before expectations or even intimacy. Back to strangers. And he'll go out, that Newfoundland man, and find a passable proximity to whomever broke his heart. She had red hair—the new woman has red hair. She worked at Eastern Health—behold—the new woman works at Eastern Health. Her name was Terry—how is that for a coincidence—the new woman's name is also Terry. Kim knew of a man who had dated three Hilarys. This, not even a common name in St. John's, was some sort of dysfunctional feat no one spoke of in his presence. There was another man who worked at her gym, an instructor of some physical appeal, who had married two Ninas. Not Amandas or even Jennifers. Ninas. Fucking preposterous.

Kim feels confident these Hilarys and Ninas were characters on *Young and the Restless*. Or maybe *Days*. Not that Kim watched the stories much after junior high. Sometimes she felt obligated to sit down with her grandmother, but even then, the total lack of respect for the passage of time vexed her. A child of five would go on vacation in March and be reintroduced as a buxom fifteen-year-old in June. The decade of childhood skipped over due to a lack of sex appeal in the storyline. 'Cause nothing interesting or integral happens to a person during that time. Nothing that, say, shapes the kind of adult you will become and the impact you will have on the world. Nah. Forget about all that. Instead, bring the character back as a tiny teen or a shirtless heartthrob and throw them into completely unrealistic scenarios that will confuse and disappoint teenagers across North America. Like who ever gets to vacation in the Caribbean, alone, with their sixteen-year-old boyfriend? Not Kim. No, her great, dirty fantasy in Grade Seven involved a Winnebago and a boy who knew how to drive it. But really it was the introduction of the absurd *Passions*, that put Kim off soaps altogether. An appreciation for witches and mermaids became the judgmental touchstone by which Kim formed opinions of the other females in her class. Any affection for the program meant you were likely to end up in a screaming match with Kim between recess and lunch. Thinking back, Kim feels, she may have been perceived as a bit of a bitch.

These thoughts occupy her mind as she drives to the Health Science Centre in her 1999 red Volvo sedan. A car with no struts highlights every bump in the road. Apt, Kim thinks, all things considered. And she's holding her water because you are told not to make it prior to getting an ultrasound. Being filled with urine is, apparently, illuminating. Another ultrasound. How very tedious. The waiting room especially. All the older couples assuming Kim is pregnant. Smiling and nodding. Good day, love. Exciting day, love. Oh, to be young again, love.

My boyfriend left me when he found out I had breast cancer. Kim wants to say. But doesn't. Because what difference would that make. He would still be gone and she would still have cancer. These goddamn breasts of hers have been nothing but trouble since that day in Grade Nine she was notified of their existence under her purple Ikeda sweatshirt.

Jesus Kim, you got tits!

She remembers slinking off to the bathroom with her arms folded over her chest in order to confirm that she indeed had tits. To her horror, she had. All the same, she hopes they'll stay even if her boyfriend didn't. The oncologist has warned her against having these thoughts before procedures. Could impact results. Elevate her blood pressure. Yes, they're concerned now. Her medley of doctors. After years of telling her to relax: try meditation, a person with your temperament should practice yoga. That's what her doctor said when she confessed her dire menstruation worries to him. Yoga. This advice she could have gotten from the damn hippie woman next door. Or Deb. That bitch. She was always going on about finding her true bliss. Apparently, she was searching for it on the end of every cock in town. Deborah: the sluttiest slut of them all. Kim imagines holding a symposium, all the delegates, everyone, women whom Deb has fucked over. There would be a recruitment seminar where women could confide in other unknowing women that Deb had slept with their husbands, too. It would be painful, yet cathartic.

Deb hung out with the pretty girls in high school but wasn't one of the pretty girls. This, and a great deal of other things, is how she rationalizes her adult choices. Juvenile hurt feelings manifesting itself in an open-legs policy.

Kim thought she was over the whole thing with Deb. Her therapist told her to deal with her underlying feelings of betrayal. The doctor said the accumulating bile related to the Deborah situation was impacting Kim's recovery. So Kim was trying to wean herself from homicidal thoughts to airtight pity. Because

wasn't Deb pitiful, working under some misguided impression
that she could increase her self-worth by fucking other people's
husbands. As if her vagina could absorb whatever coveted quality the wife had through cross-contamination. This strategy, she
pursued with abandon.

Leslie Ann Eaten is so great.
I know, she's amazing. I fucked her fiancé after the Fur
Packed Action reunion show.

Kim knows this because Deb told her these things because
they were friends. Which Kim would in turn tell Steve in a half
laughing, "aren't you glad I'm not a dirty slut" kind of way. Little
did Kim know that this was the ruse. She was baiting her own
boyfriend. She practically put the condom on his cock. If they
used a condom. They probably didn't because they're horrible
people. Kim crying in Deb's car on Bond Street.

You're supposed to be my friend.
Yeah, you said that already.
He's my boyfriend.
He's my friend too.
We have a dog.
So?

And it was the dog that brought it all back.

Kim: driving to work one morning, listening to CBC radio,
elated. They hadn't even played *Under The Covers* yet. She was
going to be on time for work for the first time in weeks! Maybe
she would be okay. Maybe things would be alright. Peachy even.
And then, there she was. Deb. Walking Beatrice down Duckworth Street. On a fucking zip leash! Beatrice way out in front.
Enough line for Kim's dog to run out into traffic. Because Beatrice would always be Kim's dog even if she couldn't keep her
right now, even if she didn't have a yard at her new place, even
if the radiation left her too weak to take the Husky outside.

Regardless, that was Kim's fucking dog, and here was Deborah Morena, that whore, walking her all wrong. You weren't supposed to let the dog lead. The human is supposed to lead. And you certainly weren't supposed to be talking on your cellphone. My God. After all the time Kim had spent training the dog, the classes, the group walks, all the patronizing conversations with receptionists at the veterinarian's. Researching online about paw pad balms, the most efficient brushing techniques, and how to prevent ear infections. Blowing fucking coats. Kim was not having Beatrice put in jeopardy because Steve had developed shitty taste in women. So Kim pulled over onto the sidewalk, up onto the curb, jumped out of her car and took her dog back, all the while screaming her head off at the woman who had once taught her how to insert a diaphragm.

I suppose you can't walk a dog properly because you're dad left your mom too, hey Deb? You fucking cunt.

Old Daddy Deb was unable to keep his dick in his pants, either. A trait that was seemingly attractive to the women in Deb's family. Her mother had taken up with a married man shortly after Daddy Deb moved to New Zealand and didn't her sister also have an affair? Anyway, he was the reason his daughter slept with every man in town. Yup, that's why she broke Kim's heart. That's why she tried to climb into Kim's life. Because Deborah didn't want what other women had, she wanted to be other women. Like a mutant life-form surviving on the still beating hearts of anyone trusting enough to share a bathroom stall with her. And Kim was warned. Some of her friends had known Deb in high school, others in University, still others had bartended alongside her in the clubs. All were unanimous—don't trust her. But Kim defended her, asked them to like her, invited her over while she put on her make-up, was in the shower, passed out from too much red wine. Left her alone with Steve. All the time.
I just found out I had cancer!
You can't be mad at me.
I can!

We were talking about how much we loved you and-

Deb had used the information she had patiently gathered over all those years of friendship to say the exact right thing.

Oh Steve, Kim's cancer is going to be so hard for you.

And Steve, that idiot. He went for it. Knowing that Deb's low self-esteem would also enable him to shove it wherever, probably also played a part, and for that, Kim had only to thank herself. Oddly enough, Kim had often warned Deb that she would eventually sleep with the wrong woman's husband and have to leave town for a while. Kim had been that wrong woman. This part she didn't see coming. In retrospect, she should have. When Deb asked Steve to lend her money rather than asking Kim. When he was jealous Deb had slept with that coke dealer. When he said Deb could do better. Steve had meant himself. They probably did stuff in her house where she slept...while she slept. Or in her kitchen where she made food that she ate with her mouth. Or in front of her dog. Kim hates them both.

Still, Kim didn't think they would call the cops about Beatrice. She knew she would have to give the dog back, what with Steve being an asshole. Kim would have never gotten mixed up with him if half of her friends hadn't moved to Korea the semester before she finished her history degree. They couldn't wait for her, oh no. They couldn't serve another deep-fried anything. One more onion ring would have sent Ellie over the edge. Acting as if jobs in Seoul would run out. Sure. Kim had been on Dave's ESL, the jobs will never run out. They would be learning English in Korea forever. Ellie could have waited for her. What's another four months of waiting tables at Jungle Jim's compared to a year's worth of stories retold forever that Kim is not in.

And the CBC radio DJ hates women.

Of this, Kim is certain. He plays that horrible song again while she is circling the hospital parking lot. There are old

men smoking in pajama bottoms near the door. There is a very pregnant woman yelling at her husband to park their massive truck. Now! Yes! Like that! Do it goddamn it! Have you never fucking parked before? Kim turns the radio off the moment she recognizes the melody. Then turns it back on to override her memory of the song. She puts on a talk station and tries to focus her thoughts on senate reform while she circles a third time. She won't be late for her appointment. She knows this 'cause they always book with a buffer of forty minutes. At her first appointment, she spent over an hour staring at a dead mouse under a chair. She took pictures of it on her phone and texted it to friends with clever quips about the state of health-care in Canada. Finally, a nurse appeared and placed a sheet of printer paper over the flaccid creature. Kim commented that a sheet letter sized paper would hardly fix the matter. The bulky nurse replied curtly that it wasn't her job and Kim lamented the state of the world. Not my job. Not my problem. Every man for himself. And the whole damn boat is sinking.

There is a kind of man that romanticizes despair. Collects records and pontificates on the contributions of dead musicians long overdosed. The forty-something man who listens to Morrissey on a summer day, while completely ignoring the elder music statesman vilely comparing eating burgers to raping children. These men enjoy hearing that miserable song first thing in the morning for sure. Maybe the DJ is one of these men. As if telling someone to call their girlfriend somehow lets you off the hook. Robyn is one smug bitch. And that Wainwright missus should know better after what her mother went through. Appalling, Kim thinks as she finally parks her car. To betray your mother like that.

Kim's own mother is a mover of furniture. She'll put the sofa across doorways. Place the television in front the window. For a change, let's try it for a change. This being something she can change. A room in her life she can physically exert herself over. Phoebe Whalen will dominate the side-tables with her petite, five-foot-two frame. She will abandon functionality to have things a different way, if only briefly. This usually starts in the evening, in the winter more often the summer, fall more often than spring. Phoebe's family, having splintered off to their preferred screens, are beckoned back after the sameness of the scene laid out in the living room has overwhelmed Phoebe to motion. She starts pulling on the arm of the sofa, dragging it across the blush-coloured carpet, feeling eased with every bead of sweat. She recruits everyone to move chairs, dust surfaces, hang frames. Half way through, her family suddenly halts to survey the damage; wing back chairs are abandoned in the center of the room, a piano bench is adrift far from the keys. The Whalens grieve the loss of their comfort, being uprooted like this on a Tuesday evening. You had to get at this tonight, had to, Scott Whalen grumbles at his wife as she vacuums indentations from the rug. It grows late before every piece snaps back together. Snaps back together. And everyone agrees, on their way to their respective beds, that they indeed prefer it this way. That they are glad they changed it. The furniture.

Phoebe buys everything pink now. Refuses to purchase the alternative because it doesn't contribute to her daughter's recovery. Kim doesn't want pink power tools. She has no desire to go on walks. She may hurt the next woman to post a make-up free selfie on Facebook and she fucking hates running. Kim has tried many times to get fit with Ellie. And Kim has hated every second of it, even though, she occasionally still goes to spin class. Regardless, she will not be pulled into the sea of positive vibes that washes over people at these crooked fundraising events. She will not sing fucking life affirming ballads as if there wasn't a lump in her right breast just below her nipple. She had asked Steve to look at a new mole. Was this always here? How am I supposed to fucking know? Who else would? she asked. He told her to see a doctor. So she did.

When Kim was a little girl her favourite pencil crayon was a prefect blend of salmon and coral, a light pink exterior with a deep pink lead centre. She would only allow her most special friends to borrow this colour. Her cousin Ellie and a boy she liked with ginger hair. Kim's fascination with colouring had forced her mother to inflict a strict no lending policy. Leads were expensive. And then somewhere, at some point, for whatever reason, Kim became aware of how desperately she did not want to be a girl. Did not want to like girl things. Would rather play with boy things. She took the perfect pinks out of her pencil case and hid them in her night table. She would have shared them with her sister if she had one. Or a brother even.

She doesn't hate pink anymore, but she refuses to eat chicken in support of a cure. Kim doesn't say this to her mom when she brings home KFC though because Phoebe is just trying to cope. Kim's cancer is not a couch she can shift. And she can't go to the hospital anymore either. That wasn't working out. Phoebe had planned on taking her daughter to treatments. She wanted to be the person waiting for Kim. But the first time a balding woman had started up a conversation, Phoebe had too quickly declared that she didn't have cancer. It was her daughter. Not her. The realization of what she was implying was devastating enough. Then, on her second visit, another woman forged ahead in an attempt at sisterhood while Phoebe pretended to be engrossed in quitting smoking brochures. No one in the family smoked.

What kind of cancer does she have?
Breast cancer.
But what kind?
There is more than one kind?
Oh honey...

And there started Phoebe's education and ended her trips to the waiting room. Kim's father usually drives her. Or Ellie.

Steve's grandmother around the bay calls Kim eight times in two days. Kim does not phone the woman back because she is tired and depressed about her hair. Finally, the old lady resigns herself to leaving a message on voicemail pleading with Kim to call her. Steve's nan starts off the call by informing Kim that he has a new girlfriend. Another one. Not that loud woman. Nobody liked her. Kim makes her disinterest in Steve's love life well known to the elderly lady in words that make her feel empowered and ashamed. I mean, my God, did she call Kim to give updates on her horrible grandson? No, no, no. Indeed, she never.

The new girlfriend is pregnant see and allergic and they're after posting your dog on the KGGG.

And Kim is hysterical. Is it not bad enough that there are cells inside her breast threatening to escape and invade the rest of her body? Is that not enough? At thirty-six years old? Kim calls her father and they go fetch the dog named after another dog in Steve's favourite film. Phoebe will feed the dog while Kim is in chemo if she has to. Her father will walk the dog every damn day if he has to. Ellie says she will come on her lunch break to check on them if she has to. Everyone will monitor the situation if they have to. Hell, Phoebe suggests they move back home while Kim is in treatment. Bring the dog. Even though Phoebe worries about her hardwood and thinks she will have to hang a door to the fine dining room where the nice plates are kept. Phoebe will not walk the thing though. Leash or no leash. Too big. But she will also not have her Kimmy's heart further harmed. She daydreams about the things she will say to Steve when she runs in to him at the grocery store or the bank or wherever it is awful people go.

Kim becomes obsessed with Susan Komen, the breast cancer beauty queen. Specifically, the mistakes the Komens made. Kim won't make those mistakes. She will have the mastectomy. She will stay alive. She tells her parents. Phoebe cries at the thought of Kim never making milk, worries that no man will want her, fears she will not feel pretty. Phoebe doesn't say any of these things. Just that she is afraid. Kim's dad doesn't say anything, he cannot talk about Kim's breasts even in the abstract manner of disease. He takes Beatrice for a walk instead. Because this is helping. The dog needs to be walked and a calm, well-exercised dog can provide comfort to his child. He wonders why they only had one child and returns to find all the furniture in the middle of the living room floor. Phoebe and Kim: not speaking to one another.

She says she's taking her tits to Mexico! Mexico!

Like a crazy person, Kim has decided to go on a beach vacation before she loses her hair and her right breast is lopped off. Her parents are beside themselves one minute and onside the next. The sun, the drinking, the men. Mexico is dangerous now. There are drug cartels! Phoebe declares they won't watch the dog one day and then immediately takes it back. The furniture doesn't get returned to any feasible floor plan for over a week. Kim moves into the spare bedroom in the basement through the downstairs door to avoid moving in through the main door. That seems much too head on, too forward, and permanent. Beatrice digs up a rose bush on their second day and Kim packs her clothes for Mexico. Phoebe secretly repacks the bag while Kim is at work. Ellie is coming, even though she is six months pregnant and jokes her figure will make other tourists uncomfortable. The cousins hold hands on the flight. Like they did when they were little girls.

Kim has promised herself she will ask Ellie questions and listen to the answers. Really listen. The last eight months she has been living in a fishbowl, only vaguely aware that the lives of her loved ones have continued. Secretly, somewhat betrayed by this fact. She has missed birthday parties, weddings, a housewarming, two art openings and a book launch. She has interrupted conversations about the fear of childbirth and dismissed Ellie's husband getting laid off. She has responded to every crisis or concern with at least you don't have breast cancer, at least you don't live with your parents, at least you have a husband. She has been a bad friend to everyone and a hateful daughter. So Kim has outlawed discussions on cancer and Steve while they are in Tulum. She will focus on long-winded explanations of Leon's career path and she will care, goddamn it. She will offer to read cover letters and indulge Ellie in detailed descriptions of post-childbirth hemorrhoids. She will not complain about her cousin's pregnancy farts, she will not make fun of Leon's health food blog. Or, at least, not very aggressively.

Tulum is not the final *tit hurrah* Kim had in mind. Every sunbather is an affront. The urge to run up and down the coastline squirting sunblock over their browning bodies is hard to repress. Then, there are all of the smokers hauling on their sticks before burying them in the sand. Stop now, she wants to scream, while you still have a chance! But worse still are all the beautiful breasts. Everywhere. She spends one whole day imagining what she will look like after the surgery, drinks too much and makes out with a Mexican bartender. This makes her feel like a sex tourist from Quebec. Which makes everything worse. Ellie tries to comfort her with tales of sour relationships long past, but it doesn't work. Kim is adamant that it's not the same.

Getting your heart broken when you're twenty-two and gorgeous is nothing like getting fucked over when you're almost forty and losing you tits, Ellie!

And Kim is right. It's not.

She calls her mother to check on the dog more than is normal, knowing full well she's roaming. She drunkenly asks to speak to Beatrice. Kim makes her mother cry by ranting about life expectancy. Kim's middle-age is over before her mom's. It's not fair. Kim will never be a great beauty, she will be as flat chested as a man, and bald before her dad. She spends a whole day replacing the word changes to stages in a David Bowie song. She sings the ode to swollen lymph nodes over dinner and feels a little triumph when her cousin cries. Kim is making everyone cry because she's angry even though she doesn't want to be. She recounts a story of Ellie stealing her super powers as a child while playing make-believe. You would say you could fly and then I would say I was invisible and then you would say you could fly and were invisible because you're greedy. You have to get everything. I get nothing.

Leon tells Ellie to come home right now. This kind of stress isn't good for the baby. But Ellie says she can't because they're like sisters.

When Kim finally returns home from Mexico, there is a Subaru in the driveway. Her dad says that single gals need all-wheel drive to, you know, help them get up the hill. This is a revelation and as close as they come to discussing the marble inside her breast. Kim also discovers her mom has learned to put marijauna into everything: chili, shepherd's pie, homemade bread, beans. Keeping weight on is very important Phoebe chides. This from the woman who calls drugs, of all kinds, *dope*. Phoebe has been baking *dope* into everything. The kitchen is full of berries, broccoli, garlic, green teas, and tomatoes. There is flour everywhere. Phoebe has also joined an online support group for family members of breast cancer patients. She explains to Kim that she has reconnected with a former student who recently lost her mother and that it has been really helpful for her journey. She thinks she will be better equipped to help Kim now. To take care of her.

Phoebe has been emailing an oncologist in Toronto that was a friend of Aunt Sharron's in college. In love with her actually, but that's another story. He's going to look through her file and give them a second opinion because some of these doctors are just butchers. Kim is tired. There is sand in her lady bits and Beatrice is eye-balling her brownie in all too familiar manner. She considers chastising her mother about the dangers of chocolate. She decides against it. Instead, she sits on the tiled floor and listens to Phoebe wax on about the latest developments in research. Her mother's baking is effective, she thinks, as she runs her hand along Beatrice's back. Great clumps of fur fly off. Beatrice's blowing coat has a never-ending supply. It all seems never-ending.

THERE'S A FISHHOOK
IN YOUR LIP

Modelaine doesn't even know how to look sexy. Matthieu has told her this many times. He has asked her to at least try as she steps out of the black, lacy underwear bought especially for him. But Modelaine ends up looking foolish and feeling self-conscious around the lean Montrealer she has taken for a lover. His parents own her building. He lives on the first floor as a care-taker and for this he does nothing. Modelaine pads around the apartment as Matthieu sleeps. She stands to the right of a picture window facing the park. She finishes herself with a wet finger all the while imagining this was her picture window facing the park, her apartment. Once she dared mention this to Matthieu after washing his bedsheets. I could live here, with you, always wash the sheets for you, she said. Matthieu sneered and made some remark about his apartment tumbling down the Human Development Index, off-handedly joking that it would take more than some earthquake and mumbling *fucking refugees*. She left and stayed away for three days.

But Modelaine's apartment on the third floor is crowded and forever smelling of cooking poultry and sweat. Uncle becomes

99

increasingly discouraged with his job, screaming at the television as if he alone was paying more for gas and Poor Aunt complains of a toe lost their first winter in Canada. Poor Aunt hadn't the proper footwear (*who could know what January was like*) and she hadn't the Metro fare either. She was forced to walk in white canvas tennis shoes that barely got her home. Poor Aunt bawling when Uncle slowly removed the frozen white canvas, screeching, *I can't feel them, they are someone else's feet, don't touch them, they will crack!* She bawled and bawled for hours.

If only she weren't quite so dark, Matthieu once said, while she sat smoking, naked on his living room floor, sliding grime out of the tile grooves with her fingernails. If only you weren't such a lying sack of shit, Modelaine has thought but never uttered, for fear of having her apartment privileges revoked. What's worse is that, in a way, she hates that she enjoys his appearance: his clean, trim body; his tight, curly, dark hair. Matthieu's lashes cannot be denied as they tip toward his pale, white eyelids. She wonders if French men curl their lashes and promises herself a search through the medicine cabinet for the device after he passes out. Modelaine can usually guess how many cans of beer it will take. Most nights are four can nights—tall ones with European sounding names. These are easy nights—lazy, warm in the living room in front of the television, snow falling outside—kinds of nights. Modelaine does not know what Matthieu has to be unhappy about and yet she senses his low-mindedness; his need for the dullness of alcohol. True sadness can't afford drink, Modelaine thinks, as Matthieu drains another can while complaining of his wasted potential. I could have been anything, he says, anything.

Though not all nights are easy nights. Some nights are twelve or fourteen-can nights. Many trips to the bathroom. Rough sex from behind and taunting with a fishhook in his lip and a crescent moon under his nose. Once, he was eight cans in when he started after her being infected, accusing her of having something he would not name. All you Haitians, he said, are like the plague. She responds that the Governor General is Haitian and he said it's the Quebecois side of her that is the Governor General. Modelaine thinks it's impossible to reason with the white dragon, and calls him a jerk in Creole. He tells her to speak real French or not to fucking speak at all and she stands in the doorway quietly crying, all the while willing herself not to. She knows she is ugly when she cries, Matthieu has told her as much. She bites down hard on the inside of her cheeks and remembers dirty starving children, some of them her own cousins. Anything is better than having to go home, she thinks and goes to the kitchen to mix a double gin and tonic in a short glass.

You're not too bright are you? Matthieu asks when Modelaine does not make his omelet the way his mother does. She wants to ask him if there is only one way to cook eggs, wants to demand how she would know how his mother makes an omelet. Wants to scream that she is hungover, too. But instead she says nothing. Instead, she watches him scrape the eggs she so carefully prepared into the trash. She will not start an argument. She will not tell him to go fuck himself in any number of languages. She will remain quiet, smile, she will bat her deficient eyelashes and arch her too-black body toward sexiness because if she doesn't, if Matthieu stops wanting her, then she will have to leave his apartment. Poor Aunt is going through an awful time upstairs and Modelaine wants nothing at all to do with it.

A cab driver has been stabbed in their neighbourhood and now Poor Aunt will not let Uncle work—will not let him leave the apartment. She is afraid he will die and she will be left to freeze in this horrible place. She dreams about her feet: brutal, cold nightmares where she cannot remove the white canvas tennis shoe without removing a foot. She screams at Uncle, declaring that broken children and the gangs of Soleil were still far better than being stabbed in some Northern wasteland. At least they were warm! Modelaine doesn't agree, but like most things, says nothing while Uncle paces the tiny apartment yelling that they will probably elect that damn rapper. That his poor, ignorant countrymen will never learn from their mistakes. Modelaine is determined to learn from hers.

Not all rice comes from Miami, Modelaine. Tabarnac. He is elbows deep into a six pack when he asks her to tell him about her home. She is suspicious of Matthieu's intentions, but happy to speak all the same. She explains that Haiti's food comes from the States and he is astounded by her stupidity. Matthieu seems very confident about his worldliness even though he has never travelled outside of Quebec. Most people are Catholic, she offers. Most practice Voodoo, he counters. Voodoo comes from a word meaning dancing, she informs. It's all glass eyeballs and wax dolls down there, he jeers. Matthieu knows more about her home, based solely on who he is and she wonders why he asked her in the first place. He reams off statistics, the numbers turning to bile in his mouth as he pours beer after beer down his throat. He is wearing that sinister moustache again and Modelaine senses things will come to a head. Matthieu, with his shiny nose and piercing words, will punish her for avoiding her family troubles, for hiding out on the main floor where everything is Canadian.

She tangles her arms around her body, trying desperately to look sleek and appealing. Matthieu touches her neck each time he rises to the toilet, resting his large palm along it lengthwise on his way to the kitchen, the heat a comfort, the weight a threat. Modelaine feels that tonight he will be somewhere between kind and barbaric. As if he can't make up his mind which type of lover he should be. This suits her intentions and she allows his fingers to linger over her soft throat. She smiles at him and remembers piercing the tiny holes, each layer of protection against her invasion faulted now with the irony of a safety pin. Modelaine wishes for a chocolate-coloured daughter with long French lashes as the toilet flushes. She considers the incisions as he burps in the hallway and stares out the picture window facing the park while he searches the fridge for another can. She thinks she'll probably put up curtains.

A CLOSET FULL OF BRIDESMAID DRESSES

Shawn never finishes the food on his plate. Doing so lacks self-control and, besides, it seems vulgar to be so hungry. Instead, he leaves a small portion to assert himself. Like a cat. It never occurs to him to do things for others. Or to do things he doesn't wish to do. Sadie finishes every mouthful for starving children in Africa. She told him this once and he remarked snidely that her logic was absurd. Sadie's mother hated wasting food and so never cooked enough when Sadie was a girl. Though a liberal and educated woman, her mother often declared the largest portions were for Sadie's father and brother. This caused Sadie to eat quickly. A get-it-while-you-can mentality ran through her even at the dinner table. Shawn doesn't understand this having grown up Catholic, middle-class and a man.

Shawn works in telecommunications and takes wedding photos in the summer. Impatient brides call him looking for their photos, but Shawn will get to it only when it suits him. He doesn't understand the anxiety around photos that won't change from one month to the next. He would prefer not to photograph these milky, doe-eyed women, but it pays well even at his bargain price. Shawn would prefer to photograph landscapes and food, which cannot express disappointment. Women, he thinks, have a natural tendency toward disappointment that they bring out in one another when they gather in groups. Women would be happier if they spent less time together talking; comparing their spouses like substitute cock measures. Because that is what they are doing, in Shawn's opinion, when they wax on about their husband's inadequacies, or crow about how lucky they feel. Merely trying to measure a moving, unattainable cock. Impossible.

Sadie sometimes acts as Shawn's assistant. She carries the tripod and tries to keep her suggestions to herself. Maybe by the lake or just beyond that clearing, momentary envy of the whole affair overwhelming her to eventually suggest. Each time she does put in, Shawn shoots her a sideways glance of remorseless contempt. She is undermining him, invading him. She never allows him a moment of attention and yet, is always staring at him. She is infuriating. He is often infuriated. Sadie once said that his capacity for rage was startling. This, of course, made him very angry. But that was years ago. When Sadie still believed one day they would get married. These days she feels like the last morsel the cat left on the plate. To prove a point.

Shawn is forever proving points. Like not getting married is a point he's proving. Or having kids with Sadie. He already has a kid, he would say, when she would mention that she might, maybe, someday want one. But that was ages ago, too. Sadie is almost forty now. All that done and over with; the wedding, the family, the house, the dog. Instead, she gets to be the girlfriend babysitter in an apartment with a rabbit. Yay. Not that she doesn't like Shawn's son. She does. It's just that he is a constant reminder. Every time Shawn makes a concession for the boy, Sadie loses something she wants. Her objections are met with silence. So Sadie apologizes for no real reason, because she is too old and tired for all of this now. All of that.

Sadie spends hours on the Google Flight search engine.

Shawn practically growls at her when he catches a glimpse of her computer screen. Her wants are an affront to him. He says, what are you looking at now? The question is laced with lighter fluid; he is an arsonist. Sadie is dry timber. A mere faggot. This has also taken years to achieve. Stick skinny. The fabricated jokes about her chocolate drawer, her imaginary late-night overeating, her greed, her hunger, had finally driven her to emaciation. The final straw being his sister's third pregnancy. Everyone cooing over how thin she managed to remain even at full-term. Such good genes. Not like Sadie's fat genes, not fit to reproduce. In a last attempt to find some worth, she quietly stopped eating. She tiptoed to the scale so as not to disturb anyone. Shawn still tells her she sounds like a football team when she climbs stairs. The lightest she has ever been still inconveniences him when he is having a lie-in till noon or taking a birthday nap.

Shawn once dated an artist before she became semi-respected in certain Montreal circles. Shawn says "dated" despite their having been together eight years. Sadie and the artist once accidentally stood naked, shoulder to shoulder at the gym, neither acknowledging the other woman's presence or the tension. Both pretending not to sneak glances. Sadie ached to speak to her, to ask her about the younger Shawn she had left, but mostly she wanted to know if it still hurt. She also wanted to declare that she had resisted, that she had tried to reason, that she wasn't a failure for having stayed. His mother often wondered aloud how she could live with him, a man like Shawn. Though this was not directed at him, he was perfect. Obviously, exceptional. Even Shawn's most recent ex was higher in the hierarchy having produced a grandchild. An indestructible link. Unlike Sadie who was clearly exhaustible.

Sadie didn't know she was a bad driver until she started driving Shawn to work in the morning. This was shortly after she moved into his house. His house being a fact he repeatedly raises no matter how much she contributes to the mortgage and bills.

105

Shawn believes Sadie neglects chores to bitch about him to her girlfriends on the phone in her spare time. Sadie doesn't have spare time. She is engaged every minute of the day—even if it's just to worry. And Sadie doesn't call people that often anymore. Instead, she makes lists of chores that get longer every year. She will keep house better than any other woman ever. She has no children and, therefore, no excuse. This, like her weight, is a trump card to play. Her busy is not as busy so she must fill it in order to maintain some equality with friends she barely sees. Poor Sadie, they say at their play dates over take-out coffee, poor Sadie must be lonely.

Sadie spends most of her days off in an anxious haze. She no longer knows what to do with herself. She tries calling a friend, but gives up moments into the conversation because she's an inconvenience. She can tell this by the screaming and barking in the background. Shawn had told Sadie they could get a dog once. She had threatened to leave again. She had packed her clothing into plastic blue containers and put a damage deposit down on a horrible basement apartment by the mall that she didn't want to live in. She would have lived there, though, if Shawn had not said they would get a dog. So Sadie searched the Internet for the puppy that would be right for them. She talked to dog owners at the dog park. She stopped people on the street.

But Shawn rejected all of the puppies she presented. Sometimes he suggested a dog breed that Sadie would then in turn reject because it didn't fit the agreed upon requirements: they were searching for a shedless, barkless, digless dog that wasn't too big, too small or too womanly. Sadie explained blowing coats, nail care, size and life expectancy multiple times before she realized they weren't getting a dog. They were searching for the perfect dog and would continue to do so until it became embarrassing. The perfect dog was like the marriage, the kids and the travelling; another means of running down the clock waiting for the right time. Something to talk about with her friends when they had time to talk.

Once upon a time, Shawn had hinted at a different future with Sadie. In this future he gave her the things she wanted. But he never had the extra money for a ring, all dogs were dirty, and he didn't really like kids anyway. He liked his own and his sister's, of course, now that they were here. But he didn't, in theory, like any children that he might have with Sadie. Sadie's loud, sensitive, fictional children were cast as potential threats to his happy solitude. They were the villains in the hypothetical story that was never realized. Only in Sadie's mind did they have names and features. Only in her mind and when she drank too much white wine, which commonly occurred when she got up too early. Shawn was irritated when she got up too early or too late. Sadie hadn't figured out the precise right time to rise. This: another constant mystery in her life with Shawn.

Sadie's brother is marrying a doctor. Their father is delighted. Doctors are in big demand; Canada's ageing population means greater job security, her father informs them on every single visit. He is forever looking at doctors' wages on the Internet. Shawn likes to turn the conversation back to Sadie's brother who manages a warehouse of some sort in a Montreal suburb. This occupation is far less grand and Sadie's father is never too keen to discuss it. He will manage the occasional positive remark on his son's employment before excusing himself to go check on the fire. Sadie's parents still have a wood furnace; it's a point of pride for her father. He can still get his own wood and save them a fortune, even in retirement. Shawn thinks this is environmentally irresponsible...and cheap. What's more, he finds the heat itself unclean, overbearing, unrefined. He can hardly manage to stay awake after dinner. Shawn hates watching television with Sadie's parents. He does so begrudgingly and only because he needs Sadie to go to his parents' house to keep up appearances.

Sadie has been secretly saving money. Squirrelling it away. She has accepted an ESL position in the Republic of Georgia. She plans on disappearing after Shawn's fortieth birthday. She knows this is a touch dramatic, but she doesn't care. She hasn't done anything of any effect for years. She'll make up for it in one gesture. This is the thing unattached women her age can actually do. They can pull up roots because there so few roots to pull up. She belongs to no one, is a part of nothing. She can wander without worrying whether it will scar the children. There are no children. Not even a dog to abandon. And Shawn will be fine. He will meet someone before the summer's end. A bridesmaid who will likely be impressed that he is a photographer. Maybe they will fall in love. Maybe it will all be different.

ULTIMATUMS GROW
WILD IN THIS PLACE

There is a man at work who is nice to everyone.

I have to remind myself of this or I become delusional. When he hovers in the doorway, while I stretch, I have to calm myself. Because he's just looking. His eyes are just open. They happen to be pointed in my direction. That's all. He's making small talk. Avoiding vocal warm ups. He has told me as much, this man. And I return his chatter until I find some pretense to leave the room. I am always ending conversations with catty remarks and fleeing. Often to nowhere.

Stratford is a small town with few places to hide. It's pastoral Canadiana. And it's stifling. Americans in sun visors take promenades through the garden. Actual Cadillacs slowly creep along the downtown streets. School groups arrive in air-conditioned buses to admire the swans and dose the students in cultural heritage. They reek of high-mindedness and pheromones when they depart. There is a piano in every home. There are a marble staircases and pashmina sales. The playwrights are awkward and the actors break out monologues in the one bar we all visit. Everyone secretly loathing each other while they hug hello or kiss good-bye. The stench of uncertainty. Encounters in stairwells end with sundresses hiked much too high up. The introduction of hip bones. Lust pressed against a vending machine. We're all driving something here. But ticket sales are not brisk and the whole town is holding its breath. Shakespeare would have fucking despised it. The economy of it all. The desperation. The antiquing.

The man was added to Titus after our Demetrius got offered a small speaking role in the new Marvel film. All those men in tights. He walked in, the man, and shook hands with everyone like a gentleman from a bygone era. It was quite a shock. I felt quite shocked. I hoped some small crisis would prevent him from shaking my hand. But it didn't. I stopped breathing when he stepped in front of me. Grinning. He does a lot of grinning. I had to take his hand for fear of looking like a germaphobe. All phobias are frowned upon in the theatre. I reached out and slid my hand into his and became keenly aware of the temperature difference. He is considerably warmer than I am. And I promised myself to not touch this man again. Ever. Touching him would be dangerous. I knew right then, that first time we made eye contact. But I told no one. I started to tell everyone. But I stopped.

Our Lavinia is having a meltdown. She does not approve of the direction of the rape scene. As if any one would approve of such a grizzly scene. But the actress playing Lavinia thinks it has been cut short. That this pivotal moment in the text requires further examination. We need to open this up more, our Lavinia says, it's the inciting incident. And it is. I am sitting on the floor, scrolling through text messages growing in domestication. Did you call about the insurance? Do we have a plan for supper? Don't forget to feed the cat. The man sits next to me humming, and peeling a small orange. A tangerine, maybe. The scent is astounding. From now on, he will smell like citrus. Or citrus will smell like him. I can see the orange, or tangerine, stain the skin between his thumb and forefinger. Tracing the lines in his hand. I can't abide the feeling of citrus on my skin. I eat apples instead because they are so tidy. It doesn't bother the man though; the citrus stains. He handles his sticky skin with a generous sense of ease. I decide to let this conversation unfold naturally. I will not impose anything on it. Don't lead, I tell myself.

The man is talking about his kids. He has many. It's sweet. He's a thoughtful father. Then he mentions his wife, she's driving him crazy. And then he says, ex-wife. Soon to be ex-wife, he says. And my abdomen opens up, the blood warms the centre of my body and it floods my spine. I have a hot tailbone. I am so happy he is getting divorced. I hate that I am, but I am. I am overjoyed at this man's failed marriage. I force my mouth into a straight line. I hold it. Alert. But the man can see the pleasure in my eyes. The effect of knowing this information has registered. He exhales and walks away to place peels in the garbage can. Lavinia rages against the injustice of a painless rape. Titus is meant to be savage. It's not conclusive, she yells. The director has started to become annoyed. He is glaring at the stage manager to manage his stage. We wait for heads to roll. What could be more conclusive than getting your fucking tongue ripped out? he demands. And I can think of a couple of things.

The man returns. It's a calculated return. He's going to ask. I know it. I have been waiting for it. Imagining what I would say. I have been rehearsing this next bit for rehearsal. So what about you, who's your partner? I don't say any of the things I intend on saying. The enlightening things about relationships being complicated. The leading things about the human heart. All of this nonsense seems beyond anything my mouth could ever project into a room. Instead I say, I have been married for a year. He pulls more information out. Also an actor. He wants more. We met at theatre school. More. A happy wife is a happy life, I say, like a fucking idiot.

My wife is not happy.

I escape to the adjacent costume bank, stand behind the Victorian gowns and slowly exhale into the heavy velvets until my heartbeat returns. It could not have gone more poorly. Now the man, who is nice to everyone, thinks I'm the prick. Every cast has one and now, he thinks, it's me. He thinks I don't care for my wife. He thinks I'm straight. Jesus. Jesus. Jesus. I worry that other cast members saw the exchange. Or heard it. Hearing it would be worse. The incredible hesitation in my voice. The desire to not reveal any information about Leanne. The desire for her not to exist. Maybe I am the fucking prick. I know I probably am. As well as I know that I have to remove myself from my marriage before I do something scandalous. Before I break my wife's heart.

The thing is, I'm gay, right?

I know this. She knows this. It is known, but never referenced. We have chosen to ignore my feigned bisexuality because it doesn't fit into Leanne's love story. She'll barely acknowledge past boyfriends. She'll discredit my sexual orientation with a flick of her wrist. Everyone experiments in college, it's practically expected, she says. Even I went down on a woman while in Regina that one time. We were on tour in the prairies. There was nothing else to do.

Sometimes I feel like Leanne has trapped me. That she caught me in my youth. I needed a roommate. She had an extra room. We were both lonely. It was easy enough. She was there. I was there. Already in the house. Moving out would have been a lot of effort. So I let it happen. Then I kept letting it happen. But Leanne's ultimatums grow wild in this place. At first, she demanded that we get married. She lay out her reasons like a buffet. I had only to choose one. And they all seemed so good at the time. Support. Partnership. Shared equity. And we loved each other, right? So we did. She did. She married us. She arranged it all. Our union forged on the fact that we liked the same television shows and had no other prospects. Leanne, convincing herself that my participation in intercourse proved I wasn't gay, that reaching around and giving her a hand demonstrated my compassion. Attraction. Desire. She never considered where I was reaching from. Or why.

Now she wants a baby.

Says her womb is taunting her. Says it's different for a woman. She speaks of her own expiration date like she is yogurt in the fridge. And I'm thoroughly revolted at the thought. Not of being a father. No. But of making a baby with Leanne in our bed of lies. Yuck. I feel certain that the ultimatums would divide and spread over every inch of my life until there is nothing left of me. See here: species formerly known as Trevor, currently covered in crocuses after years of persistent tending. Gardener: one Leanne, formerly held position of friend/girlfriend, currently known as wife. Also, known as fag hag in certain circles.

I am consumed with leaving Leanne. And not speaking to the man at work.

These are the only two things I can focus my thoughts on. They share a precarious relationship. I remind myself that I was unhappy before the man showed me a kindness. Before he knelt by my side, popped a piece of chocolate in his mouth, and talked to me quietly about the creative process. I wanted to lean in, and lean back, so I sat stock still. I felt like a mouse in the kitchen. Stunned steady by the presence of a threat. Leanne is the one who is actually threatening me. She says she will sue me for breach of contract. I say I will counter sue her for entrapment. Our house is not a friendly place. All the doors are closed. Inside rooms, bedrooms and offices, the den. Inside, we plot against each other. How we will get our way. Leanne paints the guest room the lightest shade of peach I have ever seen and I am keenly aware that the clock is ticking down. She says she will find someone to put a baby inside her. And I believe her, as sure as I believe that it will not be me.

The man at work has said laughingly that I will give him a heart attack. I accidentally call him sweetheart.

It's ridiculous. I start auditioning for other shows. I call my agent. I tell her to disregard our previous conversation regarding my level of comfort at the festival. I tell her I need a change. Yes, I will travel. No, we do not need to discuss this with Leanne. But my agent is also Leanne's agent and she tells her. Life at home has taken a rather sardonic twist. The wife is desperate. She has been letting Edgar Son of Gloucester drive our car. The man at work mentioned it while we shared a cigarette alongside a chip wagon. Hey, isn't that your car? Who's that driving it? I thought of saying, the father of my wife's future children? Or, the boy my wife is using to make me jealous. But I didn't say that. I said, some little shit Leanne is hanging out with. This, again, makes me out to be the villain. And it also makes me sound jealous. And I am jealous. The man has started counselling with his soon-to-be ex. Not soon enough, if you ask me, but no one does.

They're working it out for the sake of the children.

I get on Grindr again in the hopes that this will prevent me from touching the man at work. It doesn't. Instead, one day, I peel the sticker from my apple. I lightly press it onto his cheekbone. I rub it over the bone just slightly, rocking it back and forth, because I need to touch this man's face. And he allows it. Watches me doing it. Waits. I tell him he must have been made in the USA and slink away like a sentimental asshole. What am I doing touching this man's face? Gawd. Grindr though, Grindr only confirms that I am not one of those gay men. I am too softhearted for fucking behind local elementary schools. I think, this is why people oppose adoption. That, the violent tendency of our sex, and envy. I tell Leanne I went bareback and she pretends not to hear me. Pretends not to see me. Pretends she isn't present. Because this is a conversation we have had. A long time ago. About protecting one another. I can see a chunk of her heart slide off like ice falling from a berg. Less of her is visible. But there is something monstrous floating underneath. One night, before sleep, she says, you don't love me anymore.

I don't correct her.

Titus tells his sorrows to the stones, while I whisper mine into the living room rug. I have taken to lying on the floor whenever Leanne is not at home. I stare at the ceiling, the light fixture we hung together, and think of my impending homelessness. I try to mobilize myself. I try to create motion. I will be a man of action. But I am frozen in place. I am held to that rug. I press my face into it. I can smell cigarette smoke. Leanne has taken up smoking. She says she will forgive herself for it later. That she will forgive us for all of this later. But right now, she is full of hate. She carries it into rehearsal; she is a spite-filled fairy. And people have begun to talk. There are rumours around the festival and Leanne is looking shell-shocked. The skin on her face is hauled tight over her cheekbones. I catch a glimpse of her in the bathroom mirror while she is unaware. I watch her run her fingers along her rib cage, strumming her bones like a harp. She is playing at being a human cannibal. She is eating away at herself. I make a meat pie, but Leanne will have none of it. She refuses any offering. Because she knows I want to leave her. I force-feed myself the entire pie. I leave not a crumb on the plate. A wedding gift from my sister who cried the day we were married. Saying through her wet mascara, Oh Trevor, I think you are making a terrible mistake.

I am dogged in my appetites. There is nothing Leanne can do to deter me. I secretly separate our books on the shelves. I do so in the morning while she is sleeping or when she is out with Edgar Son of Gloucester in our car. This young man thinks he is the hero in our story. And I let him think it as long as he keeps Leanne distracted. He is a mere catalyst. He absorbs her for a time. But I know when she finally takes a run at him, he will be barreled over. My sweet wife has a salty side and that pitiful boy is going to find himself brined. But I can't waste an ounce of concern for him. I have to save it all. I am banking it for the end of the run. I am biding my time. I move into the peach bedroom and watch a lot of porn while I wait. Because I am a gay man married to a beautiful woman with a lingering infatuation for a straight man at work. For fuck sakes. I worry about myself after I jerk off. I worry that there is something very wrong with me. Not for being gay. No, I am all about that. I am fucking resolute. I intend to suck a cock as soon as I change my address, if not before. No. I worry I have tipped something over inside me. That my messy heart can never be cleaned up. I worry that I have broken myself. I tell my sister I want to end my marriage. She says Leanne will be out for blood. She tells me to lawyer-up. So I do.

I throw myself into combat. I will murder everyone on this goddamn stage. Fuck Colm Feore and fuck Anthony Hopkins, too. No one gets to have a monopoly on pain. So I share it around. I am generous with my vigor. I tap into my rage. This is an emotion I can work with. The fight choreographer is delighted! He recommends me for a role in the new Batman. There are no lines attached and I am happy to be mute. I have nothing to add to any of this. He keeps calling it a reboot and I imagine re-soling my shoes while passively lurking around on Grindr some more. The new Grindr guy is ridiculously hot. He fortifies my efforts. He doesn't believe in shirts or pants, apparently. And I don't believe in staying in a loveless marriage. So I make phone calls. At the *Midsummer's Night* opening, I kiss my wife on her cheek. She goes in to kiss my mouth. But I avoid. This is the worst thing I have ever done to her in public and the wound shoots straight through to her heart. She is porous. Everything soaks in and she looks thoroughly stained. I feel guilty. But also reassured that I am doing the right thing for us both. Because Leanne deserves a man who can savour her. And so do I.

Titus opens and is sublimely horrific. We celebrate the violence. We are jubilant about our gory tragedy. Our Queen of Goths rejoices with cocaine and there is a smallish quarrel backstage. I lose sight of the man during the skirmish. I text his phone. He doesn't respond. I set out to look for him. I catch a glimpse of Leanne in her clingiest red dress. She is holding a glass of white wine by the stem. She is snapping her fingers for a word. I will miss this about her. But I keep going because I have already left. I search the dressing rooms. There is much merriment but no man. I search the lighting booth. Still no man. I am ashamed of myself for the search but I have to keep looking because I have a sense of something. And I am going to face it. I have been blindly wandering around and now I want to see where I'm going. I hear moaning coming from the orchestra pit. I stop. I close my eyes. And consider. I choose to push on. I just force myself to keep going forward. I am a man of action now. This next bit will move me through to the other side. It will convince me. It will teach me a lesson. I walk quietly toward the pit. I step down. They come into view. He has both hands in her hair. He is guiding her. She is allowing him to do so. She is taking him over, deep inside her mouth. She uses her hands to pull him along. They are pushing each other somewhere. There is expectation in his shudder. They know where they are going because they have been here before. Often. She licks, sucks, pulls and presses. Intent. Driven. And I cannot look away. He cries out. And she giggles. Wipes her mouth with the back of her hand. They are pleased with themselves. These two. Their dirty little secret. Because this woman who made the man at work come in her mouth, this woman is not his wife.

This changes nothing. The next day, I move out.

A DOG IS NOT A BABY

Hazel promises herself that she will be more talkative the next time someone calls the house. She will contribute more than a list of the food she ate throughout the day. Egg sandwich for breakfast, warmed up some leftover soup for dinner, might put on a box of them chicken nuggets for supper, a slice of fruitcake for lunch. Her grandchildren will know the meals she's talking about because they know, not because they refer to their meals by the same names. No, all of Tiffany's meals are referred to as "snacks". Steve don't even think about food as a meal because he is married, and Martina's dinner is called lunch. For this, she goes to restaurants with her girlfriends and pays a swarm of money for spicy carrot soup. Burn the mouth right off you. Martina and her single ladies will discuss which dance to attend on Friday night as if it's a serious, grown-up topic. They won't discuss their husbands and children because they don't have any. They won't worry about what to make for supper because there's no one to cook for anyway. Supper is not even supper. It's dinner.

And there's no meal before bed for any of them. Hazel thinks it's no wonder they barely sleeps. Tiffany spends her evenings in food-free libraries, Steve passes out on the sofa as soon as the new baby is down and Martina doesn't eat after eight o'clock as a rule. She's watching her figure. This is a permanent position; the only one Hazel's twenty-nine-year-old granddaughter can manage to secure. Mind you, there are lots of teaching jobs around the bay Martina doesn't want. How will I find a husband out there, she asks, as if there was never a man born outside of St. John's worth marrying.

No, she would rather spend her evenings balancing plates on her forearms and asking other, married women if they would like pepper on their macaroni. Not macaroni. Pasta. Hazel finds it hard to remember all the words for stuff lately. They keep changing and no one tells her. If it wasn't for the damn television she wouldn't even know. Pasta, they call it now. There are a swarm of different kinds named all according to the shape as far as Hazel can tell. Her new favourite is the little bow ties, but they hardly ever has them on sale at the Co-op. Hazel's middle daughter, Joss, is forever keeping on to her mother to buy stuff regular price.

Never mind what's on sale. Buy whatever you want, Mom.

Hazel tells Joss she does buy whatever she wants and what she wants is a plane ticket home for Tiffany. And a new loveseat for the family room. She really wants a new loveseat. Joss thinks food is more important than furniture. She's after teaching Martina that, too. But it's not taking. Martina doesn't eat anything for breakfast either. By the Jesus, it's a small food window that Martina has open for herself. Drinks coffee and water all throughout the day though, which causes her to pee more often than her granny. This is a lot of pee as Hazel is forever running to make her water. Everything gives her loose bowels these days. Tiffany chastises that she doesn't eat well, doesn't eat enough vegetables, but everything brightly coloured goes right through Hazel. Her body is too old to grow accustomed to spinach now. They never even had spinach when she was a girl. The only greens they had came from turnips and even those give her gas. She can hardly stand herself after eating them. She has to leave rooms. Tiffany claims you can retrain your bowels. Yes, I suppose, Hazel thinks. But who wants to be at that? Besides, she's already seventy-three. How old do they want her to get? Acting like they want her to live forever. Sure, none of them calls her now!

No. No. Stop that. Hazel has to remind herself of her earlier oath.

If she starts thinking on how the phone never rings now, she won't be able to be conversational when it finally does. Instead, she'll respond with a series of grunts. Maybe make an offhanded remark on how she might as well be dead. Tiffany will feel guilty, her mother Margaret won't even notice, and Joss will say, it's a wonder anyone calls her at all.

What would anyone want to call you for? You never got anything pleasant to say sure.

Josslyn doesn't understand Hazel. None of them do. Not Margaret or Sarah neither. Only Martina is like her at all, but not in the any good ways. No, Martina somehow managed to inherit all of Hazel's bad qualities. It's right peculiar. And they all blames that on Hazel, too. It's somehow Hazel's fault that Martina is right preoccupied with how she looks. Hazel only said not to get fat. She didn't say to stay skinny as a rake. It's not the same thing. She said it to Tiffany too and Tiffany don't have what Joss calls a perverted relationship with food. Besides, it's true. Fat girls can't have any nice clothes. It's too dear. You can only have nice clothes if you're small. Hazel was only trying to help, trying to give her granddaughters some advice. Sure, Martina will never be able to afford any big sizes if she works at a restaurant her whole life. Hazel wishes she would find a nice man and have a couple youngsters. Knock off that old waitressing. That's for girls with empty heads. Martina is too clever to be at it and looks don't last forever. No. Hazel thinks she could die if she knew Martina was settled away. Then she wouldn't have to spend the whole day trying to figure out something to do. Sometimes, Hazel regrets not building their house alongside the store.

She didn't want to live right in the community. That's what she told their daddy, Freeman, before he started building the new house. Didn't want to live right broadside the shop. She said it was dangerous with all those cars and trucks. One of the youngsters was liable to get run over in front of the gas pump. Freeman said he didn't think there was cause for concern seeing as how they had always lived right in the community, but Hazel couldn't be talked around. Truthfully, she wanted to live off clear the road so as to discourage visitors. People were forever dropping by unannounced. Ruined her whole day. Freeman would pull a bottle of rum out from under the sink and they would end up staying all evening or till the bottle was empty. This is why Hazel never allowed Freeman to keep full bottles in the house. She insisted he pour half that old poison into an empty bottle and store it in the shed. Having to trudge through the drifting snow would usually scare him off fetching a second or third bottle. Hazel thought she could discourage this kind of nonsense-drinking by building handier to the treeline. Then, whenever someone wanted to come or go, she could confidently rely on it being too far. Too far. Nope. You don't know when the weather will puff up. Too far, Free. Too far, Sarah, Margaret and Joss. Too far. Gonna have to stay home with your mother. Hazel wasn't going to make it easy for any of them to leave her.

The same logic motivated her to insist Freeman store his rifles under the southwest corner of the house. The ammunition was stored under the northeast corner. You see, Freeman, brave as he was, loathed that crawlspace and would only attempt to gather the guns if absolutely necessary. Hazel claimed that this safety precaution was taken for the children. Another one of her half-truths—the girls would never have been so bold as to finger their daddy's guns. No. It was Joe Butler shooting his face off atop the fish plant three winters prior that was Hazel's honest motivation. She figured, she'd make Freeman work for it if ever he got any foolish ideas. Dragging himself along the ground would give him time enough to have sober second thoughts about poaching moose or shooting Marg's dog. Whatever the case may be.

Freeman's kind heart didn't always extend as far as the rabbit dog who never caught a rabbit and stole chicken off the kitchen counter. There was also Sarah, who did not project much authority as a child and was often the victim of the beagle's thieving. And Free had never shot a dog before. It was Hazel who had to throw the kittens in the brook that time. Sure, Free felt guilty over drowning mice in a bucket! Lord reeving. She knew her timid husband would be racked with guilt if ever he did shoot Trifle while in a temper. Leave it to Marg to name a gun dog after her favourite desert. Jesus. Hazel sounded starved to death every time she called the beast to come in from out doing its business. Marg was after making the animal right tame, too. Sleeping in the house all night, feeding it cream of wheat in the morning. The dog thought she was people cause of Marg's humanizing. They were the only family in the cove who let their dog on the bed. Everyone does it now, but back then it was practically scandalous. Dirty old dog in the house, Free's mother would mutter at Hazel. Dirty old dogs.

Broke Marg's heart when that dog got run over like that. Some Jesus idiot on his way to the rink left her there to deal with it, so he wouldn't miss the first period of hockey. As if that was reason enough to abandon a hysterical twelve-year-old girl to scrape her little dog off the shoulder of the road. A bit of community hockey. My gawd. Hazel's eyes well up even now remembering Marg carrying Triffie home in her arms. Blood all down the front of her grey Grenfell coat, the dog's back leg dangling. Oh my, what a vision. And there were no vets around then. The poor thing was suffering. Hazel used a feather pillow off the settee after the girls bawled themselves to sleep and buried the miserable creature in the frozen ground. That was the last dog they had. Hazel wasn't going through that horror show again—no, not for nothing. Sarah's got three Bichon Frise now. Pretty little things they are, goes out in the yard all by their lonesome. Got an invisible fence, Sarah do. But a dog is not a baby.

Hazel got a visible fence. Best decision she ever made, putting that fence up when the grandchildren came along. Safer. No playing outside the fence. Nobody else's youngsters playing inside the fence. They would've ruined the grass. All those little legs trampling around. Better yet was when they added the bridge. Fully enclosed. So it was like Martina, Tiffany and Steve were inside when they were outside. Blow the smell of house off them, it would. But right safely like. Martina, though, that little streel, would still manage to attract all kinds of random youngsters. Conduct games through the balcony wall, across a yard, and over a fence. Always getting around Hazel, Martina was. Never listened, not even when she was a baby. Insatiable. Was always hungry for more. More food, all kinds, more people, noise, affection, light, wind. Wild as the hare. Swallowed her own baby ring. Hazel had to pick it out of her diaper. Not Tiffany though. She was some good baby. Just put the bottle in her mouth and go on. Feed herself, Tiffany would. Had to though, on account of Margaret having to work them ridiculous hours over to the plant. Used to think bad hours was an inconvenience back then. Work any hours you can get now, even though their daddy thinks it's not right what the plant owners are doing with them Chinese workers.

They all thinks their daddy is perfect. Always did. The whole lot of them could find no fault in Freeman. He was the hero. And what did that make Hazel? No one ever thought for a minute how exhausting it was for her having to play the bad cop all the time. Having to discipline the works of them cause their daddy didn't have the nerve for it. Sweet, they said, so sweet. And kind. Oh yes, that was their pop. Nan though, Nan was worse than the villains on the television; worse than people on the Detroit evening news. Nan who made them all bologna sandwiches while they watched *Spiderman* and still manages to get the stains out of their fancy clothes even though she disagrees with women drinking. My Jesus, Martina must be the clumsiest drinker in the world, what for all the red wine stains she gets on her skirts. Must turn after her daddy—her pop. Her pop. Freeman is Martina's pop. Hazel does that a lot these days. Says *your daddy* to the grandchildren instead of *your pop*. She knows the difference, oh yes, she knows the generations apart, but your daddy just pops out. Like breathing. She says it without effort. Tell your daddy, get your daddy, your daddy said. Your daddy, your daddy. Freeman, Freeman, Free.

Steve's wife likes to strip the new baby down to his diaper. Got all this beautiful baby clothes but no sooner is he dressed, then she or Martina or Tiffany got all the clothes stripped off him again. Hazel worries he'll freeze his little toes off. She is constantly putting his feet up to her mouth so that she might blow warm air on them. Martina laughs at her. Tells her it's not like back in the old days when it was cold in the house. They got electric heat now. Steve's wife laughs, too. These young women think Hazel's foolish. Oh Nan, Martina says, oh Nan. This is why Hazel doesn't want to go back to Martina's. On account of her thinking her grandmother is foolish. Like once, Hazel told Martina she had to be mindful that she didn't get carried away with too many houseplants, cause they used to say houseplants will use up all your oxygen. Martina blew hot tea out her nose. Not good tea, either. Some flavourless tea. Herbal. Oh yeah, the hot water went all over the table. Oh Nan, oh Nan. Apparently, Martina learned at the university that plants were good for the air in your house. Hazel was just telling her what they used to say, is all.

I'm just telling ya, maid.

A lot of what they used to say is wrong. That's what Joss says. That science has proven a lot of these things to be incorrect. Joss also says that you can't always believe the television news. This is the most frustrating thing for Hazel. She spent the first thirty years having to listen for second-hand information 'cause she never learned her letters very good. Then they got a radio. Before long, people said everyone on the radio was telling lies. So they got a television. Now everyone on the television is telling lies. So the truth is on the computers. Or so they say. But there are all kinds of reasons why Hazel is not getting a computer. They're still pretty dear. Not as dear as a new wing chair from the catalogue, but more dear than a new television. And Hazel wants an HD one now, 42 inch. High definition. See right up their noses on *Young and the Restless*. Tiffany used to have a television that she kept in a linen closet as if it was a dirty secret. When her pop saw it, he thought it was broken. So he offered to fix it. That's how Free is, you don't have to ask. He offers. Like a gentleman. But Tiffany told her pop that it was okay, wasn't broken. Free didn't understand. How could she watch it in the linen closet?

Hazel worries that Tiffany is too much for the quiet. Always reading books. People inclined to be to themselves always has emotional problems. Thinking too much. Tiffany wouldn't have time for emotional problems or thinking too much if she had a couple little babies. But Tiffany would never put anything fit on the poor youngster. She thinks babies wants to be stretching all the time. Thinks that all the precious little baby clothes is constricting the growth of their limbs. They all wants great big feet now.

Remember when you used to make us wear little shoes to stop our feet from growing, Nan?

If Sarah phones, Hazel is going to say she's sorry for saying she wanted to slap her that time in the car. She's going to just say it right fast, get it over with. Cause she wouldn't really slap Sarah. She hasn't slapped Sarah in forty-odd years. And she wouldn't have slapped her at all if Free would have done it. And it was Sarah's own fault that last time. Hazel told her not to take her braids out at school or use anyone else's comb. There was lice going around. But did Sarah listen? That she never. Come home with her hair flying. Like Hazel never said a thing, like half the cove wasn't going around with their heads scratched off. So Hazel slapped her. Not right away. Like four days later when she had to burn all the beautiful crochet pillows off the beds. Them pillows had taken her ages to make. She was so proud of them. And then Sarah had to come home and rub her lousy head all over everything. Not to mention all the screeching they did. Margaret was the worst. Bawling her head off cause she didn't like the smell.

It's burning, you're burning me, Mom! You're burning me to death!

Enough to break your heart, it was. And Hazel hadn't slept a wink for days. She would sit up all night and crack louse eggs between her forefinger nails while they slept. It was the only time she cursed their beautiful, thick, black hair. Into the late hours she would move around the room from bed to bed as they would become restless. On the second night, she wept. On the third, Freeman came in and starting cracking eggs, too. On the fourth day, she slapped Sarah for taking her braids out again. Free was after offering to give them the belt but the girls knew that was an idle threat. Finally, Hazel couldn't stand it. Here she was after burning her lovely throw pillows in the wood stove while Sarah was flicking around tossing her hair. They were never going to get rid of the lice behaving like that. And Hazel regretted it almost as soon as she'd done it. While doing it.

And she regretted suggesting she would do it again when her youngest daughter dismissed her in the car that day. Hazel saw the hurt flash across Sarah's face before she turned to look out the window. None of Hazel's girls could ever hide anything. Open books, the lot of them. Almost two hours later, Sarah calmly told her mother that she was no longer permitted to speak in such a manner. Things had been right strained ever since and it was Hazel's own fault. Why had she said such a thing? She had been uncomfortable. Hadn't moved her bowels in days. One of the dogs was barking. Motion sickness, Sarah said. She was overly concerned about the dog. But openly dismissed Hazel's cancer worries.

Mom, you always think you have cancer.

And that's true. Hazel does. She thinks she's chocked right full of it.

She also thinks Margaret will probably call after supper. The time difference in Alberta is some annoying. Hazel got to count it off backwards on her fingers, pinky finger first. Margaret says she moved out there so she could help Tiffany pay for school, but Hazel knows she went out there chasing buddy. Jake. And he's not even fine looking. And his wife was only in the ground three months before he had another woman. And he only had her not half a year before he took up with their Margaret. That's who she's gone to Calgary running after, why she left her elderly parents home with no one in the twilight of their lives. Got to pay a young fellow to help her daddy pack the wood in so she don't feel bad. Youngsters. Hazel knows they're not ungrateful. And won't fly Tiffany home for Christmas because she's not going to be here. Offered to fly her to Calgary instead. What do Tiffany want to go to Calgary for? That's not her home. Not where she grew up. Steve and Martina aren't in Calgary. They're like a brother and sister to her. Tiffany certainly misses her cousins more than she misses her mother and Jake. Like Jake and the fat man, Jake is the fat man, like on that show. No, wait, how does that go? Anyway. It don't matter because when Margaret calls this evening, Hazel is going to tell her that they are going to pay for Tiffany to come home. She and their daddy. Margaret and Jake can go on to Nashville. That's what they really wants to do. Everyone knows it sure. They're poor liars, the pair of them.

Mom, you'd think you would be happy I found someone to do stuff with.

Hazel knows it was hard for Margaret, being thrown over like that for her second cousin. Hazel told her not to go to that wedding. Only makes people pity you sure, that kind of cross behaviour. And what did she expect anyway? Lorenzo wouldn't even acknowledge Tiffany was his, so it wasn't like he was about to run out on his own marriage for a woman he claimed he never had relations with. Then him and Cindy had to go and build the biggest kind of home on the hill right handy to them. Three bathrooms is what they said, but Hazel could not verify this as she refused to step over the threshold. House warming, baby shower, funeral reception of her own aunt, no sir. Hazel wasn't about to give Lorenzo her forgiveness. That rogue. Poor Margaret had to walk by their house to get to that fish plant every day. How many Saturday evenings did she cry when Joss dropped Martina and Steve off? Wouldn't go with her sisters to the band. No. Too proud. Don't want to spend the whole night dancing with me brother-in-law and me baby sister's boyfriend. No. Too embarrassing. Rather sit at home instead and watch Disney movies with the youngsters. Make custard on the stove and read a romance novel in the rocking chair. Like an old woman. That's what Hazel used to think, her thirty-year-old daughter was older in her mind than Hazel was. But now—now she's acting like a teenager. It makes Hazel right uncomfortable.

But I don't mind, Nanny. Really. Mom's never been anywhere warm before.

Hazel decides to eat a yogurt. Her sister Marg, that Margaret was named for, used to go right back on the yogurts because someone told her they were full of good bacteria. Supposed to prevent cancer and Hazel is more scared of having cancer than dying from it. Yes my dear. Her anxiety now is another trait heredity is after blessing Martina with. Never got Hazel's beautiful legs or her lovely skin. No, Martina got anxiety so bad it causes her to unplug everything from the wall whenever she leaves her apartment. Hazel thinks this is the only advantage to living in such a small space, less stuff to unplug. Martina is worried about everything: locking the door, filing income tax, not filing income tax, driving too fast, the lugs on the tires, her cat dying in fire, student loans, not getting any substituting, getting it. Sure, Martina is afraid the youngsters won't like her clothes. Takes her hours to get dressed for a Grade Seven History class. Hazel is only worried about having cancer so she pulls the foil off the top of a yogurt.

Good bacteria don't prevent strokes, though, so it seems. And Hazel misses talking to Marg on the phone some lot. If she could talk to Marg one more time, she'd tell her that she was a wonderful sister. Wonderful.

Hazel thinks she must get Free to have a yogurt when he comes in from at the lights. This year, they're after buying this kind from Canadian Tire that clips onto the roof. Way better than that old staple gun. Hazel decides she'll fire that up and underneath the house now, too. Open the latch and give it a toss. She could hardly watch him put the lights up last year. My, how unhandy did he look? Hazel was sure he was going to come in with staples all in his eyeballs everywhere. She had to stand and watch from the porch window with the cordless phone in her hand. She didn't know first who she would call. Joss was gone to Corner Brook to visit Steve, Sarah was in Halifax, and Margaret, well, Margaret was in Calgary with buddy. Hazel decided she would have to call the ambulance if their daddy shot himself right up with the staple gun. She would knock off putting up so many decorations if it was up to her ownself but, oh no, Free was putting up lights. They're Tiffany's favourite part of Christmas.

And the phone is ringing! Now that she's on the toilet.

Oh my, she's not going to make it. Why did they buy that cheap toilet paper? You don't save any money sure, if you got to use half a roll. Whoever it is, she will call them back. Even if it's long distance: Calgary, Montreal—especially if it's long distance. Hazel hardly got her pants hauled up over her knees before she is out the bathroom door. And she knows she's not excited when she sees 403 on the Caller Id. Cause she loves her. She loves them all. Her babies, the babies of her babies, the newest one. She wishes she had more. She wishes for more time. Perhaps she will buy some of that spinach tomorrow. If it's not too dear. The frozen stuff at least.

Yeah, Margie love. Yeah, what ya got on for supper?

ACKNOWLEDGEMENTS

I would like to express my gratitude to the Newfoundland & Labrador Arts Council, the City of St. John's, the Writers Alliance of Newfoundland and Labrador, Playwrights' Workshop Montreal, National Theatre School of Canada, and the teams at Breakwater Books and Creative Book Publishing.

I would like to extend my sincere thanks to the following for their encouragement and patience: Brian Drader, Emma Tibaldo, Robert Chafe, Sam Martin, Gerard Collins, Jenny Mc-Carthy, Jordan Flynn, Kate Andrews Simms, Ed Kavangah, Micheal Winter, Joel Thomas Hynes, Shannon Lynn Hawes, Bridget Wareham, Matthew Wishart Mackenzie, Deanna Rebellato, Robert Williams, Kerri Hodder, Mireille Myrand-Fiset, Jud Haynes, Lois Brown, Jennifer Newhook, Dave Andrews, Maia Williamson, Alex Neurta, and Sasha Okshevsky.

Special thanks to my bay family; aunts, uncles, cousins – all the cousins. My grandparents, Stephen and Susan. My sisters Melissa, Chelsie and Alicia. And, of course, my parents, Della and Nelson Coles. Much love to you all.

I apologize profusely to those I forgot to thank, you indeed deserved to be thanked. I'll get you next time. Promise.

Megan Gail Coles is a graduate of Memorial University of Newfoundland and the National Theatre School of Canada. She is Co-Founder and Co-Artistic Director of Poverty Cove Theatre Company. Megan is currently working on a trilogy of plays examining resource exploitation in Newfoundland and Labrador titled *The Driftwood Trilogy: Falling Trees, Building Houses and Wasting Paper.* She is a member of the Writers' Alliance of Newfoundland and Labrador, Playwrights' Guild of Canada, Playwrights' Atlantic Resource Centre (NL Rep) and Playwrights' Workshop Montreal. Her completed plays include *Our Eliza* (Playwrights' Canada Press & Breakwater Books), *The Battery* and *Bound.* Megan is originally from Savage Cove on the Great Northern Peninsula of Newfoundland. She currently resides in St. John's where she works at Breakwater Books Ltd. *Eating Habits of the Chronically Lonesome* is Megan's first fiction publication.